Journey to Freedom

Some Histories Refuse
To Stay Buried

Brenda M. Spalding

Published by:

Heritage Publishing. US

Bradenton, Florida

www.heritagetpublishingus.com

Dedication

This book is dedicated to my friend and mentor, D.L. Havlin, who sadly passed away.

His friendship and guidance are sadly missed.

He was a notable Florida historian and gave me valuable insight when I first mentioned the possibility of writing a book about the Saltwater Railroad.

On our trips across Florida, I learned so much about the state's history and its people.

He will forever hold a special place in my heart.

Chapter One

Arrival

The moving van groans as it pulls to the curb, brakes hissing like it's relieved to have finally stopped.

I watch from the front seat of my car, fingers still curled around the steering wheel, as if letting go might send everything sliding backward—jobs, plans, the careful logic that got us here.

Across the street, the park stretches out in late-morning quiet. Manatee Springs Park. Green and ordinary and wrong in a way I can't name yet.

Eric hops down from the cab of the truck, already talking to the driver, already settled into purpose. He looks right in this moment—clipboard tucked under his arm, sleeves rolled up, new job confidence holding him upright. This move makes sense for him. It's neat. Logical. A promotion. A fresh start.

For me, it's a relocation. That's the word we've been using. Not *move*, not *escape*. Relocation implies intention without emotion. It sounds temporary even when it isn't.

I finally open the car door.

The house waits.

It's a craftsman—solid, deliberate, the kind of house that looks like it was built by someone who believed in staying put. A low, wide porch runs the length of the front, its tapered columns resting on thick stone bases. The wood siding is painted a soft, weathered green, the color of something trying not to stand out. Exposed rafters peek from beneath the eaves, dark beams against pale trim, honest and a little stubborn.

The windows are tall and deep-set, catching the light unevenly. Not modern. Not fragile. The kind of house that expects you to live inside it instead of passing through.

I step onto the porch and feel it immediately—the way the boards hold my weight without complaint, the faint dip near the center where generations of feet must have crossed. Someone once stood here every day. Someone waited for something.

"Gabby?" Eric calls from the truck. "You okay?"

"I'm fine," I say automatically. It's not a lie. It's just incomplete.

The front door opens with a solid sound, the latch firm, the hinges well-oiled but old enough to speak. Inside, the house smells like wood and dust and lemon oil—cleaned recently, but not scrubbed of itself.

Sunlight slants across hardwood floors that bear the soft scars of time: shallow scratches, darkened seams, a faint crescent where something heavy once rested too long.

Craftsman details everywhere. Built-in bookshelves flanking the fireplace. Leaded glass in the cabinet doors. A broad archway frames the dining room, inviting rather than dividing. This is a house that believes rooms should speak to each other.

I set my keys down on the entry table and feel the strange, irrational urge to apologize—for being late, for bringing boxes, for not yet knowing the place's history.

That's when it happens.

Not inside the house.

Outside.

I turn back toward the porch without thinking and look across the street.

The park lies open and wide, a sweep of green broken by trees that rise older and thicker the farther your eyes travel. The road between us feels too narrow, as if it shouldn't be enough to separate a place meant for living from something meant for… something else.

The springs are hidden from here, tucked deeper inside, but I know where they are. I've looked at the map a dozen times. Water running south. Trails looping and intersecting. History is summarized in tidy paragraphs meant to be read quickly and forgotten just as fast.

A breeze moves through the trees.

I feel it—not on my skin, but somewhere behind my ribs. A tightening. A pause. Like the moment before a memory surfaces, when you know something is there but can't yet touch it.

The sensation isn't fear. It's more than that. It's recognition. I step off the porch and cross the narrow strip of grass to the edge of the sidewalk, as if distance might sharpen whatever this is. The park doesn't change. It doesn't react. It simply *is*—patient, expansive, waiting in a way that has nothing to do with me.

And yet. Something pulls.

Not forward. Not urging me to cross the road or follow a trail. Just… attention. As if the land has turned its face slightly in my direction, curious rather than demanding.

You're tired, I tell myself. New job. New place. Your brain is stitching meaning where there isn't any yet.

But the feeling doesn't leave.

Behind me, the moving truck thuds as the ramp lowers, and cardboard scrapes. Voices call back and forth. Life asserting itself with noise and motion.

Across the street, the park remains quiet. Too quiet.

I imagine—briefly, absurdly—that if I stood here long enough, something would happen. A sound. A shift. A voice that would make sense of this pressure I can't explain.

Nothing does.

Still, when I turn back toward the house, I feel as though I'm leaving something unfinished behind me.

Eric meets me on the porch with a grin. "First box is yours," he says, handing me a small one marked **BOOKS – OFFICE** in my own handwriting.

Of course it is.

I take it, the cardboard warm from the sun, solid and reassuring. Inside are lesson plans, novels, and notes for a syllabus I haven't written yet. The tools of a life that believes history is something you study, not something that studies you back.

"Nice place, right?" he says, glancing around.

"Yeah," I answer.

And it is. The house fits. The porch fits. The street fits.

It's the space across the road that doesn't.

As I carry the box inside, I feel it again—that sense of being observed without judgment, of standing at the edge of something patient and profound. Not hostile. Not welcoming. Aware.

I set the box down in the study, sunlight catching the dust motes in slow, careful spirals, and tell myself I'll walk in the park later.

That I'll learn its trails, read its plaques, fold it into the background of my days until it becomes just another view from the porch.

I don't know yet that this place will not fade into the background.

I don't know yet that it has been waiting.

Only that when I close the front door behind me, the house settles with a sound like agreement—and across the street, unseen and unremarked by everyone else, the park holds its breath.

Chapter Two

Before the Fire

Before the raid, Angola smelled like woodsmoke and river grass.

Morning came gently there. It slid in on mist rising off the water, softening edges, forgiving the night for being dark. The springs fed the river, and the river fed us, and everything else followed from that simple truth.

I woke to sound before light—women laughing low over cooking fires, children's feet thudding across packed earth, the scrape of paddles being lifted and set aside.

Someone always sang. Not loud. Not for show. Just enough to remind the day it was welcome.

Angola was not hidden as people later claimed.

It was *placed*.

Tucked where water branched and doubled back on itself, where trails meant something only if you already knew how to read them. We didn't vanish into the land. We learned how to stand with it.

I rose from the pallet I shared with my brother and stepped outside while the air was still cool. Dew clung to the grasses, soaking my ankles. Smoke curled upward in lazy threads, carrying the smell of cassava and cornmeal.

"Josiah," my mother called, already working the pot. "You're late."

I wasn't. But my mother liked to say it anyway.

"Yes, ma'am," I answered, grinning as I crouched beside her to stir. The wooden spoon was worn smooth from years of hands before mine. That mattered. Everything that lasted mattered.

Around us, the settlement moved in practiced rhythm. Men checked traps and nets. Women braided hair, traded cloth, and passed babies from hip to hip without breaking conversation. Children were everywhere—too many to count, too many to name all at once, which meant they belonged to everyone.

Angola was built that way on purpose.

If one person fell, another stepped in. If one family lost, another fed. No one asked where you came from first. They asked what you needed.

Some of us had come from Georgia. Some from the Carolinas. Some from places we no longer named because naming them hurt more than it helped. Some had arrived by water, thin and shaking, guided by people who knew the coast and trusted it.

The Seminoles came and went as easily as the breeze. Not visitors. Not hosts. Neighbors. They brought news, traded goods, and laughed at how we worried over the weather that never quite did what it promised.

They called this place strong. We called it home.

By midmorning, the sun burned off the mist, and the work began in earnest. I helped repair a canoe that had scraped limestone too hard the week before. My brother patched a roof with palm fronds, his hands quick and sure. Someone argued good-naturedly over where to plant next season's crops.

"Too close to the water," one voice said.

"Water's why we're alive," another answered.

Both were right.

Angola held more than bodies and buildings. It held intention. Every choice here was deliberate—where we built, when we moved, how much we took. We had learned what excess invited. We had learned what attention cost.

Still, joy found us.

It found us in the afternoons when work slowed and children splashed in the shallows. It found us in shared meals, hands, and laughter. It found us in the evenings when elders told stories—not always about escape or suffering, but about tricksters and storms and foolish men who underestimated women.

At night, the fires burned low and steady. That was when the talk sometimes turned quiet. Not fearful—never fearful—but watchful.

People spoke of movement. Of routes. Of water that carried you farther than roads ever could. Not as panic. As preparation.

My father sat beside me one night, sharpening a blade he didn't need sharpened.

"You listen more than you speak, Josiah," he said.

"I like knowing things," I answered.

He nodded. "Good. Then know this. Safety isn't stillness. It's knowing when to move."

I didn't understand then what it would cost to learn that lesson fully.

I only knew that Angola felt permanent in the way good things do—not because they can't be broken, but because they are worth rebuilding.

The day before the raid, nothing felt wrong.

That's the lie people tell later—that there were signs, warnings, omens we ignored. There weren't. The river ran as it always had.

The birds sang. The children fought, made up, and fought again.

I remember helping my mother hang cloth to dry, the fabric snapping lightly in the breeze.

"You'll have a family of your own one day," she said, not looking at me.

"Maybe," I said. "If I'm lucky."

She smiled then. "You already are."

That night, I walked to the edge of the settlement and looked out toward the dark water. The stars reflected faintly on the surface, broken and whole at the same time.

I felt something then—not fear, not warning.

Contentment.

That is what silence later tried to erase most of all.

Not the suffering.

The life.

When the fires came, people would say Angola was doomed from the start, that it couldn't last. That it was always temporary.

They were wrong.

Angola lasted as long as anything ever truly lasts.

Long enough to leave a mark deep enough that even fire and paper and time could not fully scrape it away.

I did not know then how soon everything would change.

Only that when I lay down beside my brother that night, the sounds of Angola settling around me, I slept without fear.

And that, more than anything, is what I carried with me into the dark—the memory of a morning where the world made sense, and we believed it would keep doing so.

Chapter Three

The Way the Water Knows

My father did not talk about escape the way others did.

He never lowered his voice. Never glanced over his shoulder. He spoke of it the way a carpenter speaks of wood grain— something you respect, something you learn to read, something that will punish you if you pretend it isn't there.

We sat at the edge of the river as dusk settled, the day loosening its grip on heat. He had brought his net to mend, though it didn't need mending. That was his way of talking—hands busy, eyes on the work, words arriving when they were ready.

"You've heard them talk about north," he said, not looking up.

"Yes, sir."

"Freedom papers. Cities. Names you can stand on."

I nodded. Everyone had heard those stories. The land routes. The long walks through pine and swamp. The promise of lines on maps that meant something different on the other side.

"And you've heard the other way too," he went on. "The one people don't like to say out loud."

I swallowed. "South."

He glanced at me then, quick and sharp. "Why don't they like saying it?"

"Because it sounds backward."

He smiled faintly. "Backward from what?"

I didn't answer.

He set the net aside and dipped his fingers into the water, letting it run over his skin. The river carried the day's light away piece by piece.

"North is a direction," he said. "South is a decision."

I frowned. "I don't understand."

"You will," he said gently. "Because north is something other people tell you about. Laws written by men who never had to run. South—south is something the water tells you."

He motioned with his chin toward the river. "Where does this go?"

"To the Gulf."

"And then?"

"To the islands. To places with different flags."

"Different laws," he corrected. "Different memories."

I had heard whispers—Bahamas. Cuba. Places where Spanish words are mixed with English and African tongues. Places where a person could arrive broken and still be allowed to become whole again.

"But it's dangerous," I said. "Boats capsize. Storms come fast."

"Yes," he agreed. "People die."

The honesty startled me. My father never softened the truth for the sake of comfort.

"People die staying too," he continued. "They die waiting. They die believing the land owes them mercy."

He picked up the net again. "South isn't chosen because it's safe. It's chosen because it's *possible*."

I watched the water move around his wrist, dark and steady.

"Why not north, then? Why not both?"

"Some do go north," he said. "And some make it. But the north is crowded with expectation. Papers. Patrols. Men paid to look for you, the slave catchers."

He met my eyes again. "South is wide."

He told me then about the Saltwater Railroad—not as a story, not as a legend, but as a practice.

How the currents change after sunset.

How certain stars sit low enough to guide you if you know their names.

How wreckers along the Keys sometimes pretended not to see, and sometimes saw everything.

How boats traveled not in straight lines, but in patience.

"Water doesn't forget paths," he said. "It remembers everybody who learned to trust it."

I thought of the elders who spoke softly at night, of the way movement was discussed not as panic but as readiness. "Why doesn't everyone go, then?" I asked.

He sighed, a long breath that carried more weight than his words. "Because leaving costs something, too."

He touched his chest once. "You leave graves. You leave voices. You leave the certainty of knowing where your feet will land."

I swallowed hard. "Would you go?"

He looked out over the river for a long time. The light faded to copper, then to shadow.

"If I had to," he said. "If staying meant forgetting who I was."

He turned to me then, placing a hand on my shoulder. "That's the part you need to understand, Josiah. The Saltwater Railroad isn't about running away."

"Then what is it?"

"It's about choosing what you refuse to surrender."

I felt something settle in me then—not fear, not urgency. Responsibility.

"What if you don't make it?" I asked quietly.

His grip tightened just enough to be felt. "Then someone else will. And they'll carry your name with them."

That was the promise.

That no one vanished alone.

That water could carry more than bodies—it could carry memory.

That night, as we walked back toward the lights of Angola, I looked at the river differently. Not as a boundary. Not as an obstacle.

As a road that did not need to be built to be real.

I did not know yet how soon that knowledge would be tested.

How quickly would South stop being an idea and become a necessity.

Only that when my father spoke of the Saltwater Railroad, his voice did not shake.

And that told me everything about why some people chose the water.

Not because it was kinder than land.

But because it still listened.

Chapter Four

What Eric Notices First

Eric notices the change before Gabby says anything about it.

It's not dramatic. Not the kind of thing you can point to and name without sounding foolish. It's a collection of small shifts— the way she pauses at the front window longer than necessary, the way her attention drifts when she thinks he isn't watching, the way she stops mid-sentence as if listening for something that hasn't quite arrived yet.

Grief does that, he tells himself.

Grief rearranges people.

They've only been in the house a week, and it's the first real move since her mother died. Before that, everything was temporary—sublets, short-term rentals, furniture that never quite fit. This place is different. Permanent. Anchored. The kind of house that expects you to unpack everything, including what you'd rather keep boxed.

Eric leans against the kitchen counter and watches Gabby trace the edge of one of the built-in shelves with her fingers, not absentmindedly, exactly. Intentionally.

"You okay?" he asks, keeping his voice light.

"Yeah," she says too quickly. Then softer, "Just tired."
She's been tired a lot lately.

He recognizes the signs—not from textbooks, but from living inside systems long enough to know what pressure looks like when it starts working sideways.

Gabby throws herself into structure when she's overwhelmed. Lists. Lesson plans. Syllabi rewritten three times before breakfast. And now this—this quiet pull toward the park across the street.

Eric didn't think much of it at first. Everyone stares at something new when they move. But Gabby doesn't look at the park the way people look at scenery. She looks at it the way she looks at old photographs—searching for context.

At night, she sleeps lightly. Not nightmares. Just shallow rest, the kind that snaps awake at small sounds. He hears her shift in bed, hears the breath she doesn't realize she's holding.

He tells himself it's normal.

Grief plus relocation equals stress. Stress equals imagination filling gaps.

Still.

The morning she misses her turn on the way to school because she's watching the tree line instead of the road, he finally says something.

"Hey," Eric says gently, tapping the dashboard. "You want me to drive for a bit?"

She blinks, startled. "Sorry. I didn't even realize."

That's the part that unsettles him.

That afternoon, he calls his sister on the way home from work, keeps the conversation casual until he doesn't.

"She's not falling apart," he says. "Just… different."

"Different how?" his sister asks.

Eric exhales. "Quieter. Sharper. Like she's carrying something she hasn't named yet."

A pause. "Have you suggested Gabby talk to someone?"

He grimaces. "About grief? Or about the park across from the house?"

Another pause, longer this time. "Eric."

"I know how it sounds," he says. "I just don't want to miss something important because I assumed it would pass."

That night, he brings it up carefully.

They're sitting on the porch, cicadas buzzing in the trees, the park across the road a darkened mass that somehow still draws Gabby's eyes. He hands her a mug of tea and watches her wrap both hands around it, as if she needs the heat.

"You've been carrying a lot," he says. "Your mom. The move. New job. All of it."

She nods but doesn't look at him.

"Would it help to talk to someone?" he continues. "Just—check in. No pressure."

She stiffens almost imperceptibly. "I'm not breaking," she says.

"I know," he answers quickly. "That's not what I meant."

Finally, she turns to him. Her expression isn't angry. It's confused.

"I don't feel broken," she says slowly. "I feel… alert."

The word lands wrong.

"Alert how?"

She hesitates, searching for language that doesn't sound irrational even to her own ears. "Like something's about to make sense. Or like I'm standing near something important, and I don't know why yet."

Eric smiles, gentle but strained. "That's… not exactly reassuring."

"I know."

She laughs then, short and rueful. "I know how it sounds. I promise, I'm okay."

He wants to believe her. And mostly, he does. Gabby has always been the grounded one. The historian. The person who trusts evidence over instinct, documentation over myth.
But this place—this park, this house—has shifted her center of gravity just enough that he can feel it.

Later, when she's asleep, he stands at the front window and looks out across the road himself.

The park is dark, unlit, ordinary. Trees. Paths. Nothing threatening. Nothing waiting.

Still, he feels a faint unease he can't justify.

Maybe it's the house settling. Perhaps it's the weight of responsibility he feels, having convinced her this move was right. Or maybe it's something else entirely—something he doesn't have language for yet.

Eric rests his palm against the glass.

Whatever this is, he thinks, I'm not letting her carry it alone.

That much, at least, is certain.

Chapter Five

The Silence

The birds always know first.

They fall quiet the way a room does when someone steps inside who should not be there. One moment, the air is alive with wings and calls and movement, and the next it is as if the land has drawn a breath and decided not to release it.

That is how I know someone new has arrived.

The road across from Manatee Springs Park hummed with the sound of a moving truck grinding into place. The engine idles too long, coughing, unsettled. Cardboard scrapes against metal. Voices float—light, careless, unafraid.

They never hear the silence.

I stand where the trees thin and the earth dips, near the edge of what used to be Angola. The name is not on any sign now. It lives only in the ground, pressed into sand and roots and water, carried the way blood carries memory long after the wound has closed.

I have watched them come for more than two hundred years.

Families. Couples. Builders. Surveyors. Children who chase fireflies and laugh where no one should laugh. They stay for a season, sometimes longer, and then they leave with their voices tight and their eyes searching for reasons they cannot name.

I know before they do.

This one is different—*she* stepped down from the truck and paused, just for a moment. Her hand tightens around a set of keys. Her gaze drifts toward the park, toward the trees that lean together as if whispering.

She felt it. Not clearly. Not yet. But enough. That is new.

It feels like yesterday when my mother and I ran for our lives from the Negro Fort on the Apalachicola River.

Fire split the sky open that day, and the ground rose up to meet us. The sound of it never leaves you—not truly. Even now, when the world has wrapped itself in roads and houses and forgetting, I can still feel the explosion ripple through my bones.

Only a few of us escaped.

My mother clutched my hand so hard I thought she might break it. Her cries followed us into the trees—my father's name, my brother's, my sisters'. Names torn loose from the living. Names that never came back.

1816, they would later write. They always write dates as if they are enough.

We fled south after that, deeper into Florida, following rumors and the Peace River and the promise of land that had not yet learned how to betray us. Angola was a settlement of the unwanted—Maroons, they called us, as if the word could flatten what we were into something manageable.

Seven hundred of us lived there. Runaway slaves. Freed people who knew freedom could be taken back. Native Americans fleeing General Jackson and his soldiers, who burned villages and called it order. Some went farther south, into the Everglades, to join the

Seminoles. Others stayed with us because fear binds people faster than blood.

For a time, we lived in peace.

At night, we gathered around fires that kept the dark at bay, and the elders told stories meant to hold us together. Stories of survival. Of routes through the swamps where dogs lost the scent. Of water that could carry you farther than feet ever could. They spoke of a railroad with no tracks.

One train ran north, they said, where slavery had no legal hold. Another ran south, over saltwater, to the far edge of Florida and beyond to islands where freedom waited in a different language— the Saltwater Railroad.

I had never seen the ocean then. Never stood on a boat deck or tasted salt on my lips. But I dreamed of it anyway. Dreamed of buying passage for my mother and me, dreamed of a future that did not require hiding.

Dreams are dangerous things.

The woman across the road turns slowly now, scanning the trees. The birds do not return. Cicadas hold their breath. The land leans toward her, curious.

I do not reach out.

That takes strength, and I have learned to ration it. I have pushed small things before—keys nudged just out of sight, floorboards coaxed into sound—but never without cost. Memory has weight. So does grief. You do not survive centuries of watching without learning restraint.

Still, I feel something shift as she looks toward the park. Recognition.

I have waited here since the day Angola burned.

That morning arrived without warning. No birds. No insects. No voices drifting between homes. My mother did not stir her pot over the coals. Smoke did not rise. The silence pressed down until even the children sensed it.

An old man stepped out to draw water. His bucket scraped the ground. His eyes darted like prey's.

The rifle cracked. A red bloom spread across his chest, bright and sudden. He touched it with disbelief, as if it might be wiped away. The bucket fell. He followed it into the dust. Then the guns sang.

Seven hundred Maroons and Native Americans died at Angola in 1821. That is the number they argue over now. The date they soften—the word they avoid. Massacre.

I did not leave when others fled. Some souls slip free when the bodies fall. Others stay, bound by love or fear or unfinished promises. I stayed because my mother could not run. I stayed because someone had to remember where we fell.

Across the road, the woman bent to lift a box. She moved carefully, as if her body expected resistance where none should be. When she straightened, her face had gone pale.

She has been here two weeks now, and the feelings are getting stronger.

She will wake tonight with water in her dreams.

I know this because the land has already begun to open itself to her. The springs murmur louder when she draws near. The ground warms beneath her feet and cools again too quickly.

Only some can hear the past when it stirs.

Once, around the fires, an elder said certain people are born with thin places inside them. Places where memory slips through like water through fingers. I did not understand then. I do now.

The door slams. Laughter breaks the quiet, sharp, and out of place. A man's voice—Eric, she will call him—carries easily. He does not feel me. He will not, unless the land decides to punish him for standing too close. It has done that before.

I turn away from the road and face the park. Spanish moss sways like the skirts of dancers long gone. The springs breathe in and out, patient.

The Saltwater Railroad still runs.

Most do not believe that. They think routes die when feet stop walking them, when boats rot, and names vanish from paper. They do not understand how memory moves.

I have waited more than two hundred years for the right person to arrive.

The birds remain silent.

And for the first time in longer than I can remember, I feel something like hope pressing back against the weight of waiting.

Chapter Six

What the Land Knows

The silence doesn't announce itself. That's what unsettles me most about it. It doesn't crash, echo, or demand attention. It just *exists*, settling over everything like a held breath. I noticed it while I was carrying the second box from the truck—halfway across the driveway, when the cicadas should be screaming.

I stopped walking. The cardboard dug into my palms. Sweat ran down my spine. Florida in late summer has a sound to it, a constant thrum of life insisting on itself. I've taught enough regional history to know that. I've lived here long enough, too. This quiet doesn't belong.

I remember Eric calling from behind me. "You okay?"

I nodded automatically and kept moving, but my gaze drifted across the road to Manatee Springs Park. The trees there stand closer together than they should, their branches woven thick with Spanish moss that sways even when the air feels still.

I felt like I was being watched. Not in the way horror movies teach you to expect. There's no prickle at the back of my neck, no instinct to run. It's something subtler—like walking into a room where a conversation has just stopped.

Eric didn't notice. He never does with things like this. He's already planning where the furniture will go, talking about internet installation and trash pickup days—practical things. Safe things.

I envy him.

The house itself is small but solid, pale siding weathered by sun and time. It's technically a rental until we decide whether the relocation sticks. Eric's promotion came with enough incentives to make moving feel like the logical choice—more money, better hours, room to breathe after the long, grinding months following my mother's death.

Bradenton seemed like neutral ground. Close to water, far from memories.

I didn't realize land could have its own memories.

Inside, the air feels cooler than it should. Not air-conditioning, cool—*old* cool. The kind you find in buildings that have learned how to hold onto the past. I set the box down harder than necessary.

"Gabby," Eric says gently, and I hear the question he doesn't ask. Are you okay? Are you spiraling again? I had a hard time dealing with my mother's death.

"I'm fine," I said. "Just tired."

It's true enough. Grief leaves you exhausted in strange ways. It sharpens your senses and dulls them at the same time. I'd spent the last year floating through days, grading papers by muscle memory, standing in front of classrooms while my mind replayed hospital corridors and the steady beep of machines.

This move was supposed to reset things.

Instead, the longer I'm here, the more I feel like I've arrived late to something that's been waiting.

That night, I dreamed of water. Not drowning—nothing so dramatic. Just water stretching farther than it should, dark and glossy beneath a moon that hangs too low in the sky. I'm standing on a shoreline that feels familiar, even though I've never seen it before. The sand is warm beneath my feet. Someone is calling my name, but the sound dissolves before it reaches me. I wake with my heart racing and the taste of salt on my tongue.

Eric sleeps on, breathing evenly. I lie still, staring at the ceiling, listening.

The silence is back.

The next morning, I tell myself I imagined it.

That's my default setting these days: explain, rationalize, move on. I shower, dress, and drink coffee that tastes faintly metallic.

Outside, the cicadas resume their chorus as if nothing ever stopped them. The normalcy is almost a relief.

Still, when I stepped onto the porch, my eyes drifted toward the park again.

Manatee Springs Park spans a couple of acres across the road, its boundaries marked by low fencing and weathered informational signs. I read one out of habit as we drive past later that morning—dates, conservation efforts, geological features.

Nothing about Angola. I don't expect there to be. History has taught me what gets remembered and what doesn't. Still, the absence presses against my ribs like a bruise.

Chapter Seven

A Beginning

Finally, the term begins. Eric drops me off at the school just before eight. The building is low and sprawling, painted in optimistic colors meant to soften fluorescent lighting and long hallways. I've taught in places like this before. Every school carries the weight of unspoken things—teenage grief, ambition, fear. Compared to that, I should feel at home. Instead, I feel unmoored.

My classroom smells faintly of dry-erase markers and dust. I unpack textbooks and arrange my desk with careful precision. When I tape my class schedule to the board, my hand trembles just enough to notice.

First period trickles in, then second. I lecture on early Florida settlements, keeping my voice steady, my slides polished. Students take notes. Someone yawns. Someone asks about extra credit. The normal things

Then, halfway through the third period, my projector flickers. The slide freezes on a map of nineteenth-century Florida— coastlines jagged, interior blank in the way maps used to be when people didn't bother naming what they didn't value.

My mouth keeps moving even though my train of thought derails. "—and settlements like Fort Gadsden played a role in—" I stop. I didn't plan to mention Fort Gadsden today.

A student raises her hand. "Is that near here?"

"Yes," I say automatically. "Near the Apalachicola River."

The word *Angola* presses against my teeth. I swallow it back.

After class, I sit at my desk longer than necessary, staring at the frozen map until the projector hums back to life on its own. The room feels smaller, tighter. I rub my temples and laugh softly at myself.

Back home, I try to dismiss things. You're reading too much into things, I think. Classic teacher brain—always connecting dots that don't need connecting.

It happens on a Tuesday afternoon when I'm supposed to be grading. I set my pen down without realizing I'd stopped reading.

I don't decide to. I just do.

Barefoot, I cross the hardwood floor and stop at the front window. The glass is cool against my fingertips. Across the street, Manatee Springs Park lies open and ordinary—green canopy, packed-earth trailheads, a wooden sign listing hours and rules.

The boxes are still half-unpacked in the study, books stacked in uneven towers on the floor because the built-ins aren't empty yet.

The house creaks softly around me—settling sounds, Eric calls them—but they feel more deliberate than that, like the place is learning our weight.

I slip my feet into sandals and step onto the porch, the late-afternoon heat pressing against my skin. The wood beneath me is warm, familiar already. I press my thumb into the grain of the porch railing, grounding myself. I am a historian. I believe in causes, in evidence, in narratives that can be traced and cited. I move to the edge of the steps, stopping where the grass meets the concrete.

The road between the house and the park feels thinner than it should.

I could cross it in seconds.

I don't.

I find myself standing in the road without remembering walking there.

The park looms across from me, trees darkening as the sun dips low. The air smells damp, rich with earth and something else I can't name. Pressure builds in my chest. Not pain. Recognition.

I take a step forward, then another, crossing the line where asphalt gives way to packed sand. The cicadas falter. The silence slides into place around me with unsettling ease.

"This is ridiculous," I mutter. My voice sounds too loud.

Outside, the light has shifted.

Not dimmed. Not darkened. Just… angled. The sun slides lower, and suddenly the park across the road looks closer than it did this morning, the tree line sharper, more defined, as if someone adjusted the focus.

Nothing about it should command attention.

And yet my chest tightens.

It's not anxiety. I know what that feels like. This is quieter. A tug without urgency. The sense you get when you hear your name spoken softly from another room—not loud enough to demand, not sharp enough to startle, but impossible to ignore.

I tell myself I'm restless.

New job. New town. The strange disorientation that comes from knowing where you are but not yet where you belong.

Still, I watch.

The wind moves through the trees unevenly. Leaves shiver, then still. Somewhere deeper in the park, birds fall silent all at once, the absence of sound more noticeable than any noise.

I inhale and catch the faint smell of water.

That makes no sense. The springs are too far away. But the scent is there anyway—clean, mineral, edged with something old.

Memory, my brain supplies unhelpfully.

Except it isn't my memory. I've never been here before. I know, suddenly and without explanation, that this isn't about going closer. Not yet. The feeling isn't a summons. It's awareness—like being noticed by something that does not need to rush.

A laugh drifts from somewhere inside the park. A family, maybe. A child. Life continuing in ways that don't acknowledge whatever I'm standing at the edge of.

"You're being ridiculous," I murmur.

The word sounds wrong in my mouth.

Behind me, the house shifts again, a low sound like a breath taken and released. When I glance back, the windows reflect the trees across the street so clearly that for a moment I can't tell where the house ends and the park begins.

A shiver runs through me—not fear, exactly—more like anticipation without context.

This is none of those things.

And yet, when I finally turn away, the sensation doesn't leave.

It settles instead—low and patient—somewhere beneath my ribs, like a question that has decided to wait until I learn how to ask it properly.

The path into the park curves gently, inviting without promise. I don't go far—just far enough for the world behind me to feel distant. My pulse thrums in my ears. Images flicker at the edges of my vision: firelight, running feet, water reflecting stars.

I squeeze my eyes shut. "Get a grip," I whisper.

When I open them, the feeling hasn't gone. It lingers, patient.

I turn back before Eric can come looking for me, heart hammering like I've escaped something I don't understand.

Inside, the study feels smaller than it did before. The boxes look less like clutter and more like proof that I intended to stay busy, to stay anchored in paper and ink and the safety of recorded facts.

I pick up my pen again.

The words blur.

Across the street, unseen and unremarked by everyone else, the park holds steady—neither welcoming nor warning, simply present.

And for the first time since we arrived, I understand something without knowing how I know it:

This place isn't calling me forward.

It's waiting to see if I'll listen.

That night, as we eat dinner and talk about logistics and schedules, I keep my gaze fixed on the table. I don't tell him about the park. I don't tell him about the dream. I don't tell him that when I wash my hands before bed, grains of sand spiral down the drain.

Chapter Eight

She Turns Toward Me

She crossed the road today. Not far. Not deep into the park. But far enough that the land recognized her footsteps and shifted itself to meet them.

I felt it the way you think a storm is moving in before the first drop falls—pressure changing, the air thickening, the small lives going still. The cicadas cut off mid-song. The birds tucked their calls away as if hiding them under their wings. The silence slid into place around her like it belonged.

Most people push against that silence without knowing they're doing it. They keep walking, keep talking, keep living, and the land learns to ignore them. It is easier that way. Safer. The past stays buried, and the living remain untroubled by what has wrapped around it.

But she paused. She stopped on the packed sand and looked into the trees as if she could see the shape of what had happened here.

That is what startled me most.

Not that she came. People come all the time—day hikers, families with coolers, teenagers chasing each other on summer evenings. They wander through Angola without knowing its name and leave with sunburns and photographs and no sense of the weight under their feet.

But she paused like she heard something.

And the land—always hungry for someone to remember—leaned closer.

I did not mean for the sand to follow her.

That was not a trick. Not a message I shaped with intention. It is simply what happens when the past begins to bleed, and the living walk too close to its edge. A grain of sand in a shoe. A smear of river mud on a sleeve. The scent of smoke clinging to hair after a dream.

Small things. Warnings.

I have learned to watch for those small things because they are the first sign of danger.

I stayed long enough to see how this world works, how men in clean clothes can erase a massacre with a pen, how the right kind of silence can turn horror into a footnote. I watched roads laid down across memory. I watched names vanish from paper and resurface only in whispers. Some people think forgetting happens by accident. It doesn't.

For years, I believed my waiting was a punishment. That I remained because I'd failed to run, failed to save my mother, failed to buy us passage on the Saltwater Railroad. But time has a way of peeling your reasons down to bone. Somewhere along the way, I understood the truth.

I stayed because Angola could not speak for itself. And then—without warning—someone arrived who might hear it.

She is called Gabby, though I did not know her name at first. I learned it the way I learn most things now: through repetition, through the weight of a voice spoken with love.

The man—Eric—said it as he carried boxes into their house. *Gabby, you want this in the kitchen? Gabby, did you eat today? Gabby, come look at this.*

He says it like a lifeline. He does not know what he has tied to his own throat.

Tonight, she sits at a table in a room lit by yellow lamplight. The window above the sink frames the park like a dark mouth. She watches it more than she thinks she does. Her gaze drifts there when the conversation falters, when Eric laughs at something on his phone, when she stops chewing as if she has forgotten what food is for.

She does not tell him what she feels. She does not tell anyone. But she cannot make herself stop listening.

That is the danger of people like her. Once the past finds a crack, it presses in.

I have seen it before, though rarely.

There was a boy once—many decades ago—who wandered into the park alone. He had the look of someone running from a home that no longer felt safe. He sat at the edge of the springs and cried without sound, shoulders shaking. The silence gathered around him, soft as a blanket.

He looked up suddenly, eyes wide, and whispered, "Who's there?"

I reached for him without meaning to.

The water shivered. The boy's face went pale. He ran.

The following week, he returned with his father, who cursed the "bad air" and yanked him away.

They moved soon after. They never came back.

I learned then what it costs to be noticed. Not for me. For them.

So I stayed hidden. I let the land do what it would. I waited for the right kind of listener—someone who wouldn't run the moment the truth brushed their skin.

Gabby did not run until she had to. Even then, she ran like someone retreating from a cliff edge, not from a monster. She ran because her body understood danger, not because her mind believed it. There is a difference.

Now, in the quiet of her bedroom, she lies awake staring at the ceiling, eyes open too long. Eric's breathing is steady beside her. She listens to the house settling, to the hum of the refrigerator, to the distant hiss of traffic.

And beneath it all, she listens for the thing she felt in the park. Her grief makes her thin.

That is what people do not understand about grief. They think it is something that fills you up, something heavy that weighs you down. Sometimes it does. But grief also hollows you. It strips away the layers you used to hide behind. It makes you porous. It makes you easier to reach.

When she finally closes her eyes, the water comes for her again.

I do not summon it. I cannot, not the way the living imagine. But the springs remember. They remember bodies washed clean of blood. They remember boats slipping into black water beneath stars. They remember prayers whispered into palms.

The Saltwater Railroad was always more than rumor. It was a path shaped by desperate hands—canoes and skiffs and anything that could float. It was moonlight and mangroves, and silence pressed into the spaces between patrol routes. It was mothers pushing children forward, men turning back to draw dogs away, women swallowing fear because someone had to.

It was hope. And hope leaves a mark on land as surely as death does.

In her dream, Gabby stands at a shoreline again. The moon hangs low. The water glitters like broken glass. Somewhere nearby, voices murmur—not English, not entirely, not the language of now. She hears her own name threaded through it. She turns her head.

And for the first time in more than two hundred years, she turns toward me. The distance between us is not measured in steps. It is measured in willingness.

I stand where the water meets sand, where history presses its mouth against the present. I do not have a body the way I once did. I do not have breath. But I have memory, and memory can be louder than any shout if the right person is listening.

Gabby's face in the dream tightens with fear. Then softens into something else. Recognition.
She takes one step forward. The water does not reach her this time. It waits.

I feel the land hold still. I try to speak.

The effort is like pushing through mud, like lifting a stone that has settled for centuries. Still, I press one thought into the fragile space between dream and waking.
Listen.

Her eyes widen. Her lips part. She whispers into the night air of her dream, "Who are you?"

The sound of her voice hits me like wind through a door left open too long.

I cannot answer with a name. Names have edges. They are hard to carry across time. But I can give her something smaller. Something that fits through the crack she has opened. A date. A place. A warning.

The dream shudders. The shoreline blurs. She gasps—and in the real world, her body jerks in bed. Eric stirs, murmuring, half asleep. She clamps a hand over her own mouth as if to trap the sound inside. But the past has already touched her.

She sits up, shaking, and turns on the bedside lamp. Light spills across sheets and skin and the ordinary shape of a life that wants to stay ordinary. She swings her legs over the edge of the bed.

Sand spills from her hair onto the pillow. She stares at it, breathing hard.

I feel her mind fight for an explanation.

Beach. Wind. Dream.

But she knows she did not go to the beach.

She knows the wind has not been strong enough to bring sand into a closed house. She knows—deep down, the way you know when someone is standing behind you—that something crossed a line.

I should stop now. I should pull back and let the crack seal again before it widens into something dangerous. I should let her return to her safe explanations, her daylight logic, her lesson plans.

I have watched too many crumble under what the land asks of them.

But then she whispers into the lamplight, voice raw, not quite steady.

"What do you want?" The question is not aimed at her own fear. It is aimed at me.

And somewhere in the park across the road, the trees shift with a sound like slow applause.

The springs murmur louder. The silence deepens—not empty, but attentive.

Something else stirs beneath it.

Not my memory. Not the water's. A different weight. A colder intention.

I feel it turn, like a locked door recognizing a key in the wrong hand. The other one has noticed her too.

I press myself back into the land, into roots and sand and old grief, trying to gather strength for what comes next.

Because now that Gabby has heard me—truly heard me—there is no returning to before.

And the past does not easily give up its listeners.

Chapter Nine

Why We Came

I don't tell Eric about the sand. I scoop it off the pillow before he wakes fully, brushing it into my palm like it's nothing more than grit tracked in on bare feet. I carry it to the bathroom and rinse it down the sink, watching the grains spiral away. The water runs clear. Ordinary. Cooperative. My hands keep shaking long after.

"Bad dream?" Eric asks when I crawl back into bed.

"Yeah," I say, because it's the safest answer. "Just stress."

He pulls me close, warm and solid, and for a moment I let myself believe that's all it is. Stress. Grief. A move that came too soon or too late. I breathe him in and count heartbeats until my own slows. I know he loves me and the comfort of being in his arms.

Still, when morning comes, I feel like I've crossed some invisible line in the night.

The truth is, I didn't want to move again. After my mother died, I wanted stillness—something that didn't require packing boxes or learning new roads. I wanted rooms that already knew my shape. Instead, everything familiar became unbearable. Every grocery store aisle held a memory. Every drive took me past places she and

I had been together, laughing, arguing, existing in a way that felt permanent until it wasn't.

Eric tried. He really did. But grief rearranges the world in ways love can't always reach.

So when the offer came—his promotion, the relocation package, the promise of better hours and a fresh start—we told ourselves it was timing. Opportunity. A chance to reset before the weight of loss calcified into something we couldn't escape.

Bradenton wasn't special. That's why we chose it. Neutral ground. Sun and water and the quiet comfort of anonymity.

And for me, a teaching position opening midyear—Florida history, of all things. I should have laughed at the coincidence. Instead, I felt that tightening in my chest again—recognition without context.

I tell myself now that I'm projecting. Teachers are trained to look for patterns. We make meaning for a living. Sometimes we make too much of it.

Still, as I drive to school, the park flashes past my peripheral vision like a held thought. Trees crowd the road. Water glints through breaks in the foliage. I feel watched, not by eyes, but by attention—focused, patient. I grip the steering wheel harder and keep going.

My classroom smells the same as yesterday: markers, dust, and the faint smell of lemon cleaner. I start the day on autopilot, greeting students and writing objectives on the board. When I turn to face them, the words blur for a second before snapping into focus.

Early Florida Settlements: Conflict and Survival.
The phrase sits heavier than it should.

As I talk, something feels slightly off, like my voice is half a beat behind my thoughts. I catch myself saying *'we' when I mean 'they'*. I correct it quickly, but the slip lingers.

At lunch, I eat alone in my classroom, scrolling through lesson plans I've taught a dozen times before. My eyes snag on a footnote I've skimmed past every other year.

Angola: a maroon settlement destroyed during early U.S. military campaigns—one sentence. No date. No detail. I stare at it longer than necessary.

This is how erasure works, I think. Not with lies, but with thinness. With facts starved of context until they can't stand on their own.

I should close the document and move on. I have quizzes to grade, emails to answer, and a life to manage. Instead, I open a new tab.

The school's database gives me the basics—summaries lifted from older texts, all of them curiously vague. Words like *dispersed* and *engagement*. Passive constructions that neatly sidestep responsibility.

My jaw tightens. "Figures," I mutter. I make a note to look deeper later. Academic curiosity, I tell myself. Nothing more.

That afternoon, the sky clouds over with the kind of sudden intensity Florida specializes in. Thunder grumbles in the distance as I drive home, the park dark and glossy beneath the approaching storm.

I don't stop this time.

At the house, Eric is already there, laptop open at the kitchen table, sleeves rolled up. He looks up when I come in, smiling, and some of the tightness in my chest eases.

"How was your first real day?" he asks.

"Fine," I say, then hesitate. "Busy."

He nods, understanding the word means more than it says. We fall into the comfortable rhythm of dinner prep and small talk. He tells me about meetings, about office politics that feel trivial compared to the weight pressing at the back of my mind.

When the rain starts hammering the roof, I jump.

Eric notices. "Hey," he says gently. "You sure you're okay?"

I almost tell him then. About the dream. The sand. The way the park feels like it's leaning toward me. Instead, I shake my head. "I just need sleep."

That night, I don't dream of water. I dream of fire. Not the roaring kind—controlled, purposeful. Torches moving through trees. The smell of smoke carried on the wet air. I wake with my heart pounding and the echo of screams fading into silence.

The rain has stopped. The house is quiet. Too quiet.

I pad into the kitchen for water and catch my reflection in the dark window. For a split second, I don't recognize myself. My eyes look older. Sharper. Like someone who has seen something they can't unsee.

Across the road, the park is a black mass against the sky. Lightning flashes, illuminating the trees in stark white. For the briefest instant, I think I see movement near the edge of the springs—a gathering of shapes that vanish as quickly as they appear.

I tell myself it's the storm. I'm lying to myself now, and part of me knows it.

The next morning, I wake early and sit at the kitchen table with my laptop and a cup of coffee that goes cold before I drink it. I pull up county records, old maps, and scanned military correspondence.

I expect resistance—paywalls, red tape. Instead, things open too easily. That's when I notice the first inconsistency.

A date shifted by a year. A report that references Angola as active after it was supposedly destroyed. Numbers that don't line up. Casualties are reduced in later documents, then omitted entirely.

My pulse quickens. "This isn't right," I whisper.

The house creaks softly, as if settling—or listening.

I don't yet know what I'm looking for. I only know that something here has been smoothed over too carefully. Someone wanted this story quiet.

When Eric comes into the kitchen, I close the laptop too fast.

"What're you working on?" he asks.

"Lesson stuff," I say. "Florida history."

He grimaces sympathetically. "Sounds thrilling."

I force a smile. But as Eric leaves for work, a thought presses into my mind with unsettling clarity. We didn't choose this place by accident.

And whatever waits across the road knows exactly why I'm here—even if I don't yet.

.

Chapter Ten

The Clearing

I tell myself I'm only going for a walk. That's the lie I choose because it's small and familiar and doesn't demand explanation. I say it aloud when Eric asks where I'm headed, house keys already in my hand, jacket slung over one arm.

"Just across the road," I add. "I need air."

He glances toward the park through the front window. The sky is bruising into evening, clouds stacked low and heavy. "Before dark?"

"I won't be long." That part is true, at least in intention.

The moment my feet leave the pavement, the air changes. It's subtle—no dramatic drop in temperature, no sudden gust of wind—but my skin prickles as if I've stepped into a room that remembers being full. The cicadas are loud at first, then uneven, then quiet altogether as I follow the path into Manatee Springs Park.

I stop walking. The silence settles around me with unsettling precision, like a door closing behind me without a sound. I can still hear my own breathing, the soft crunch of sand beneath my shoes. Everything else feels… held.

"This is stupid," I whisper. My voice sounds wrong here. Too sharp. Too present.

The path curves gently toward the springs, bordered by palmettos and live oaks draped in Spanish moss. The moss sways even though the air feels still, long gray strands brushing together like fingertips.

I keep going. I don't know why. I only know that the pull in my chest has sharpened into something like direction. Not a command. An invitation.

The clearing opens ahead of me without warning. One moment, trees enclose me, the next, the land dips and widens, revealing a stretch of sand near the water's edge. The springs glimmer darkly in the failing light, their surface unnaturally smooth. The smell here is more pungent—wet earth, iron, something faintly acrid beneath it. Smoke.

My heart stutters. I've never smelled smoke here before. There's no fire, no camp, no sign of anyone else. Still, the scent curls into my lungs like a memory.

I take one step into the clearing. The pressure hits me all at once. It's not physical pain.

It's grief—dense and layered, pressing from every direction. My knees weaken, and I have to brace myself against the sudden urge to sit, to sink into the sand and let it swallow me.

"Oh," I breathe. Images crash through me in fragments too fast to make sense of. Fire tearing through the darkness. People running, shouting names that don't belong to me. A woman's scream—raw, unending. The crack of gunfire sharp enough to split the air.

I clamp my eyes shut and stagger backward. "No," I say aloud. "I'm not—this isn't—" The ground hums beneath my feet.

Not sound exactly. Vibration. Like something vast shifting its weight. I open my eyes. I am not alone. I don't see anyone.

There is no shape standing in the clearing, no figure emerging from the trees. But the space across from me feels occupied—attentive, focused, waiting. Recognition washes over me, startling in its certainty.

"You're here," I whisper. The words feel less like a question and more like an acknowledgment.

The air tightens. My pulse roars in my ears, but beneath it, another rhythm emerges—slow, steady, patient. The springs ripple once, then still.

I don't know why I kneel. My body simply does it, as if remembering something my mind never learned. My palm presses into the sand, and the sensation is immediate—warm, grounding, alive with a hum that travels up my arm and settles behind my eyes.

I gasp. More images—boats slipping into water under moonlight, hands pushing off from shore, whispered prayers carried by mangroves. The word *train* flickers through my mind, absurd and insistent. A railroad with no tracks.

"The Saltwater Railroad," I whisper, the name arriving fully formed. The response is immediate.

The grief surges—not crushing now, but focused, edged with longing so sharp it makes my throat burn. Tears spill down my face without warning, and I don't bother wiping them away. They soak into the sand beneath my hand.

"I don't understand," I say, voice shaking. "If you want something from me, you can't—"

The pressure eases slightly, like a held breath released. Understanding trickles in—not as explanation, but as knowing. This place is layered. Lives pressed into lives, footsteps worn into paths long erased. What happened here did not end. It settled. It waited.

I think of my classroom. Of sanitized summaries and footnotes that skate past horror without pausing. Dates soften until they lose their teeth.

"I teach history," I say, the words spilling out faster now. "If you want to be known—if this matters—I can help. But you can't keep doing this to me." The clearing goes very still.

For a moment, I think I've gone too far. That I've offended whatever holds this place together. Fear skitters up my spine, and I brace myself for something worse—for pain, for punishment, for the ground to open beneath me.
Instead, the air shifts. Not approval. Something closer to relief.

The vibration beneath my palm changes, gentling, and with it comes a sensation so unexpected it steals my breath—gratitude. Vast and aching and unmistakable.

"I don't know how," I whisper. "But I'll try."

A presence draws close—not touching, never touching—but near enough that my skin prickles as if brushed by cold air. For a heartbeat, I feel the echo of a hand near mine, hovering where my palm presses into the sand.

Waiting. The moment stretches, fragile as glass. Then something else moves. It's subtle at first—a tightening at the edges of the clearing, a sense of impatience intruding on the quiet. The warmth beneath my hand cools abruptly. The grief sharpens, turning jagged, warning flares through me.

"I should go," I say, scrambling to my feet.

The pressure spikes, not holding me back, but urging—now.

I back away from the clearing, heart pounding, eyes fixed on the dark line of trees. The cicadas explode back into sound the moment I cross the invisible boundary, their noise almost painful in its suddenness.

I don't stop walking until I reach the road. Cars pass, headlights flaring, oblivious. The world snaps back into focus with cruel efficiency. My hands shake as I fumble for my keys.

Back in the house, Eric looks up from the couch, concern etched into his face. "That was fast."

I nod, unable to find my voice. I go straight to the bathroom and run cold water over my wrists, watching my reflection with wary eyes.

Sand clings to my skin. Again.

That night, sleep comes in fits and starts. When it does, it drags me under into fragments of fire and water and voices speaking names I don't know.

Somewhere beneath it all, something watches. Not the presence in the clearing.

Something colder.

Something that does not want to be remembered.

Chapter Eleven

Bleed-Through

I wake choking on smoke. For a heartbeat, I'm certain the house is on fire—that I've slept through alarms and sirens and the moment when everything becomes irreversible. I bolt upright, lungs burning, hands clawing at the sheets.

The smell fades.

I'm left gasping in the dim light of early morning, heart hammering hard enough to shake my ribs. The ceiling swims above me. My mouth tastes like ash.

"Gabby?"

Eric is already awake, sitting on the edge of the bed, eyes sharp with worry. He reaches for me, then hesitates, as if unsure whether I want to be touched.

"You were yelling," he says. "Not words. Just—" He gestures helplessly. "Like you were trying to breathe."

I drag in another shaky breath and press my palms to my thighs. They sting. When I look down, I see why.

Fine grains of sand coat my hands, packed beneath my fingernails, ground into the creases of my skin. A few flecks dot the sheets like evidence I can't explain away.

"That's not possible," I whisper.

Eric follows my gaze. His brow furrows. "Did you go back to the park last night?"

"No." The answer comes too fast. Too sharp. "I mean—no. I came straight home from school."

He doesn't accuse me of lying. He just studies my face, and that somehow feels worse.

"You were talking in your sleep," he says carefully. "Names. And a date."

My stomach drops. "What date?" I ask, though I already know. "Eighteen… twenty-one, I think." He swallows. "And Angola. You said it more than once."

I swing my legs out of bed and stand too quickly. The room tilts, then steadies. My feet meet the floor—and I flinch. The hardwood is cool. Damp. Not wet enough to leave footprints. Just enough to feel wrong.

"I'm fine," I say automatically. "I'm just overtired."

Eric's jaw tightens. "Gabby." He's frightened for me.

I grab a sweatshirt and pull it on like armor. "I have an early day. I'll explain later, okay?"

He lets me go, but his eyes follow me down the hall, heavy with questions neither of us is ready to voice.

In the kitchen, I pour coffee I don't drink and open my laptop instead.

If I'm going to be haunted—if that's what this is—then I'm not facing it unarmed. I anchor myself to what I know. Facts. Records. Paper that can't change just because I'm afraid.

I searched Angola, Negro Fort. Early nineteenth-century Florida military campaigns.

At first, everything looks as it did yesterday: vague summaries, passive language, tidy conclusions. Then I dig deeper—older scans, marginal notes, versions uploaded decades apart.

That's when I see it clearly.

A military ledger dated *1820* is in one archive. The same event dated *1822* in another. And a third document—a scanned report with faint handwriting in the margin—where the date has been scratched out and rewritten.

1821, the ink is darker. Firmer. Intentional.

My pulse roars in my ears as I zoom in. Beneath the altered date is a note, barely legible but unmistakable.

Numbers adjusted per directive.

I lean back in my chair, breath shallow.

"This wasn't a mistake," I whisper. "This was a decision."

Seven hundred reduced to dozens. A massacre reframed as a "conflict." Names erased, replaced with statistics that don't add up.

History doesn't just forget, I realize. It is made to forget.

The house creaks softly behind me. I freeze. The sound isn't threatening—just a shift, old wood responding to temperature and time. Still, my skin prickles. The air feels charged, expectant.

"You don't want this found," I say aloud, not sure who I'm addressing. "Do you?"

The silence presses back, sharper now. Not grief. Not patience. Resistance.

The lights flicker once, hard enough to make me gasp. My laptop screen dims, then brightens again. Outside, the cicadas cut off mid-song.

Fear crawls up my spine.

I slam the laptop shut and grab my bag, shoving it inside without caring how obvious my panic looks. I don't trust the house anymore. Not with this open. Not with whatever else might be listening.

"Gabby." Eric stands in the doorway, keys in hand. He looks tired. Pale. Like someone who didn't sleep well and doesn't know why.

"I'm taking the car," I say. "I'll walk home later."

"What's going on?" he asks quietly. "You're scaring me."

I want to tell him everything. I want to dump the truth into his hands and let him decide what to do with it. But the words tangle in my throat, thick with the knowledge that saying them out loud will make them real in a way I can't undo.

"Please," I say instead. "Just trust me. For now."

He hesitates, then nods. "Call me if you need anything."

"I will."

At school, I keep my head down. I teach, I grade, I smile when required. All the while, the altered date burns in my mind like a brand.

During my planning period, I pull the document back up—this time on a public computer in the faculty lounge. I print it, my hands steady despite the tremor running through me. As the page slides into the tray, I feel it.

A presence. Not the one from the clearing. This is colder. Tighter. It presses against the edges of my awareness like a hand closing around a throat—not squeezing yet, just letting me know it could.

The printer jams. Of course it does. I free the page with shaking fingers and turn—and nearly collide with a man standing too close behind me.

"Sorry," he says smoothly. "Didn't mean to startle you."

He's older, gray-haired, and wearing a county badge clipped to his jacket. His smile is polite. Practiced.

"Visiting historian, my name is Harold Miller," he adds. "I'm doing some outreach with local schools."

My grip tightens on the paper.

His gaze drops—just briefly—to the document in my hand. His eyes sharpen, not with curiosity, but recognition.

"That's a complicated subject," he says lightly. "Angola."

My mouth goes dry.

"I didn't realize you covered it here," he continues. "Some histories are… better left contextualized."

The pressure spikes. This isn't a coincidence.

"I teach history," I say, forcing my voice steady. "Context is the job."

His smile thins. "Of course. Just be careful, Ms…?"

"Rivera," I answer.

"Well," he says, stepping back, "welcome to the neighborhood." He walks away, whistling softly.

I stand there long after he's gone, the hum of the lounge suddenly oppressive.

Across the road from my home, unseen but unmistakable, the park waits.

And beneath it—beneath memory and grief and water—something else shifts, irritated now.

I have crossed from noticing into interference. And whatever has been guarding the lie knows my name.

Chapter Twelve

What Must Remain Manageable

The historian Harold Miller does not consider himself a villain. That distinction matters to him.

He has built his career on preservation—on *context*, as he calls it. Context softens edges. Context makes difficult things digestible. Context allows the past to exist without disrupting the present too violently.

That is his job.

He sits at the long conference table with the school board members to his left and county officials to his right, fingers folded neatly over a leather portfolio that has never once been misplaced.

The room smells faintly of coffee and disinfectant, the scent of institutions that expect compliance.

"We need to talk about Ms. Rivera," he says carefully. No accusation. No urgency. Just concern, precisely calibrated.

The superintendent exhales. "She's a good teacher. Ms. Rivera came to us highly recommended."

"Undoubtedly," the historian agrees. "That's part of the issue."

A council member raises an eyebrow. "Explain."

He opens the folder—not to read, but to *anchor the moment*. Paper reassures people. "She's energetic. Engaging. And she tends toward… narrative momentum."

"That's not a crime," someone mutters.

"No," he says smoothly. "But it can become a liability when enthusiasm outruns verification." He lets that sit.

Across the table, a county planner shifts in his seat. "You're talking about Angola."

"I'm talking about *scope*," the historian replies. "Angola is a fragmentary history. Poorly documented. Emotionally charged. The kind of subject that attracts attention disproportionate to its evidentiary weight."

A board member frowns. "There were people there."

"Yes," he concedes. "Briefly. And tragically. But elevating the site beyond its current interpretive framework invites complications."

"Complications like what?" the planner asks.

The historian chooses his words with care. "Descendant claims. Land-use challenges. Public pressure to revise curricula before we're prepared to do so responsibly."

Responsibly.

He has learned that word opens doors.

"We are not saying the history is false," he continues. "We're saying it must be handled quietly. Carefully. Without creating expectations that cannot be met."

The superintendent taps her pen. "Gabby Rivera is grieving. Her mother's death was recent. That kind of loss can make people… fixate."

The historian nods sympathetically. He has already prepared this path.

"Exactly. This may not be the right moment for Ms. Rivera to engage with material that carries such emotional weight. It might be kinder to redirect her focus."

"To what?" someone asks.

"Curriculum development. General state history. Safer ground."

The planner clears his throat. "And the park?"

"The park," the historian says, "should remain what it is—a recreational space with limited historical markers. We can acknowledge *presence* without inviting excavation."

A silence falls. Not disagreement. Calculation.

He presses gently. "Once a story gains traction, it develops its own momentum. We risk losing control of interpretation."

"And that's bad?" the superintendent asks.

"Yes," he answers without hesitation. "Because interpretation without control becomes precedent."

No one likes precedent.

He senses hesitation, so he shifts tactics—not retreat, just adjustment.

"This isn't suppression," he says. "It's stewardship. We preserve what we can verify and refrain from amplifying what we cannot fully substantiate."

Someone nods.

Another adds, "We don't want controversy."

"Exactly," the historian says. "And Ms. Rivera—however well-intentioned—has the potential to create one."

The meeting ends without a vote, without a directive.

Those are the best outcomes.

As he gathers his things, he feels no guilt, only relief.

History survives because someone decides how loudly it's allowed to speak. Miller believes that deeply. Without restraint, the past becomes unruly—demanding things the present cannot afford.

Outside, as he walks to his car, the historian glances toward the park.

It looks harmless. Trees. Paths. Families.

He tells himself that quiet is not erasure.

It is protection.

What he does not consider—what he cannot afford to consider—is that some histories do not disappear when kept quiet.

They wait.

And waiting, he will soon learn, is not the same as obedience.

Chapter Thirteen

The Other One

She has crossed the line now.

Not the one between road and park—that was inevitable. Not even the one between past and present. That crack opened the moment grief hollowed her enough to listen. No, this is a deeper crossing—one with consequence.

She has touched the lie.

I felt it the instant the printer jammed.

The hostile presence does not live in the land the way I do. It does not remember mothers and children and boats slipping into moonlit water. It remembers *orders*. Ink pressed hard enough to bruise paper. Authority spoken until it no longer sounds like a choice.

It is not a ghost. It is the echo of a command.

When men decided Angola must disappear, they did not just kill bodies. They erased language. They revised the ledgers. They trained themselves to carry out their duty long after the gunfire stopped. That obedience soaked into the soil as surely as blood. That is what woke when she printed the document.

I tried to reach her then—not with words, but with weight. A tightening of air. A flicker of warning. She felt it, though she did not yet know what it was. Fear sharpened her senses. That may save her.

The man at the school—the historian—was never meant to be her enemy. He is only another mechanism. Another lever pulled by the same hand that has been pulling for two centuries. He smelled the disturbance and responded the way institutions always do. Contain. Redirect. Diminish.

She does not yet understand how dangerous that makes him. Tonight, she sits at the kitchen table with the printed page folded into quarters, hidden beneath her notebook. Eric moves around her, careful now, watching her the way one watches weather that might turn.

"Someone came by the school today," she says finally.

He stops to listen. "What kind of someone?"

"A historian. County-level." She swallows. "He noticed what I was looking at."

Eric's jaw tightens. "Noticed how?"

"He knew the date had been altered."

Silence stretches between them, thick with unsaid things.

Outside, the cicadas resume their song, too loud, too sudden.

"That's not good," Eric says at last.

"No."

She waits for him to say more—to tell her to stop, to pull back, to let the past remain safely buried. He does not. He only rubs a hand over his face and exhales slowly.

"You're in danger, aren't you?" he asks.

She nods.

He does not laugh. He does not accuse her of imagination. He looks tired and afraid and very much in love.

"Okay," he says quietly. "Then we need to be smart."

I did not expect that. I don't know what I expected, but not that. Most people demand certainty before courage. Eric does not have certainty. He has trust. That may cost him. The other one has already marked him.

It brushed against him earlier, on the road near the park. A hesitation in the engine. A flicker in the electrical system. Nothing dramatic—just enough to remind him how fragile he is. That is how it works. Fear is more effective when it pretends to be a coincidence.

Later, Gabby stands again at the edge of the park, the paper folded tight in her pocket like a talisman. She does not step into the clearing this time. She stays on the path, just close enough that the land leans toward her.

"I know you're there," she says.

I gather myself carefully. Slowly. It has been a long time since I tried to speak plainly.

You woke something. I press into the space around her. *Something that feeds on forgetting.*

Her breath catches. "It's not you."

No.

She closes her eyes, steadying herself. "What is it?"

I hesitate. Names give power. Understanding gives even more.

It is permission, I tell her. *The belief that erasure is mercy. That silence keeps order.*

She opens her eyes. "And it doesn't want me digging."

It does not want anyone digging.

The air tightens briefly, a warning ripple that does not belong to me. The other one is listening now, irritated by clarity.

"If I stop," she asks, "will it leave Eric alone?" The question hits harder than she knows.

It will always look for leverage, I answer. *Stopping only teaches it what works.*

Her shoulders square.

That is when I finally understand what she is. Not a listener. A witness.

She pulls the paper from her pocket and smooths it against her thigh. "Then I can't do this quietly anymore."

The land shivers—not in fear, but in recognition.
There will be a cost, I warn.

She nods once. "I know."

The other one shifts, coiling tighter around institutions, process, and procedure. Emails will vanish. Permissions will be revoked. Jobs will be threatened. It will not roar. It will suffocate. And it will start with Eric.

I do not know if I can protect them both.

I only know that the Saltwater Railroad never ran safely. It ran because people moved anyway, knowing what waited behind them if they stayed.

Gabby turns back toward the house, the park at her back, truth folded close to her heart.

The birds fall silent again.

This time, it is not anticipation. It is a warning.

Chapter Fourteen

What Eric Sees

Eric has always trusted patterns.

That's what his job trained him to do—systems, workflows, causes followed by predictable effects. If something breaks, there's a reason. If something goes wrong, it can be traced, documented, and fixed.

What's happening to Gabby doesn't fit that logic. He notices it first in the pauses. The way she stops mid-sentence as if listening to something he can't hear. The way her eyes drift toward the park across the road, even when they're talking about grocery lists or weekend plans.

She's not distracted. She's *focused*—just not on anything visible.

He doesn't say anything at first. Grief does strange things to people. He learned that watching her after her mother died, how she'd forget small details, how exhaustion lived under her skin no matter how much she slept. This feels different, but he doesn't want to be the guy who turns concern into accusation.
Still, there are moments he can't ignore.

Like the way the house feels colder when she's restless. Or how the cicadas seem to stop when she steps outside at night. Or the fact that his car stalled yesterday in a place it absolutely shouldn't have.

Route 64. Flat road. Recently serviced vehicle. No warning lights until they all came on at once. Coincidence, he tells himself. But coincidence doesn't explain the way his chest tightened when the engine died. Or the sudden certainty—sharp and irrational—that he shouldn't get out of the car. That something was *watching*.

He shakes the memory off as he pulls into the driveway that evening. Gabby is inside, light glowing in the kitchen. The sight of her steadies him, like it always has.

She looks up when he comes in, relief flashing across her face before she masks it.

"Hey," she says.

"Hey." He sets his keys down more carefully than necessary. "We need to talk."

She stiffens. Just slightly. Enough that he notices.

They sit at the table, the space between them charged. He doesn't bring up the car. Not yet. He starts with the thing that's been needling him all day.

"The park," he says. "You keep going back there."

Her fingers tighten around her mug. "I know."

"You don't tell me why."

"I'm trying to protect you."

The words land harder than he expects.

"From what?" he asks.

She hesitates, and for a moment, he thinks she'll shut down, retreat into the careful half-truths she's been using lately. Instead, she looks tired. Not the bone-deep exhaustion of grief, but something sharper—like someone who hasn't stopped running mentally even when her body rests.

"I think something happened there," she says slowly.

"Something that never got finished. And I think… I think it doesn't want to stay quiet anymore."

That should be the moment he pushes back. The moment he says, "Listen to yourself, or you're reading too much into this." Eric can hear those words lined up and ready.

They don't come. Instead, he thinks about the engine stalling—the flicker of the streetlights. The way the air felt heavier near the park, like humidity without heat.

"Okay," he says carefully. "And what does that have to do with you?"

She meets his eyes. "I can feel it."

The honesty in her voice unsettles him more than the words themselves. She isn't asking him to believe in ghosts or curses.

She's describing a sensation, the way someone might describe pressure or pain.

"What about me?" he asks quietly.

Her throat works. "I think… I think you're leverage."

That gets his attention.

"For who?"

"For whatever doesn't want the truth known."

The room feels suddenly smaller. Eric glances toward the window, toward the dark mass of trees across the road. He's never liked that park at night. He chalked it up to unfamiliarity, but now the unease sharpens into something more defined.

"Gabby," he says, choosing his words with care, "are you saying someone is threatening us?"

"Yes," she says. "Not someone. Something."

Silence stretches between them, taut as a wire.

He thinks of all the times he's told her they'd face things together, of the promises that felt easy when danger was theoretical.

"Then we don't pretend this is just your problem," he says finally. "And you don't go out there alone anymore."

She exhales shakily. "I didn't want to drag you into this."

"You didn't," he says. "It followed you. There's a difference."

Later, when she's asleep—or at least pretending to be—Eric lies awake staring at the ceiling. The house creaks softly around him. Outside, the cicadas fall silent one by one.
He listens to the quiet. For the first time since they moved, he understands that what's happening isn't about belief. It's about attention. About what notices you when you start noticing back.

His phone buzzes on the nightstand, an email notification. From work. *Subject: Compliance Review – Immediate Attention Required.* Eric's stomach drops.

Across the road, unseen but undeniable, something tightens its grip.

And Eric understands, with a clarity that leaves no room for denial, that whatever this is—it has stopped circling.

It has chosen its pressure point.

Chapter Fifteen

The Names Begin

I stopped using official channels. No emails. No database logins. No requests that leave a trail I can't erase.

The moment Eric shows me the compliance notice on his phone, something clicks into place—sharp and undeniable.

This isn't about curiosity anymore. It's about control.

I wait until the house is quiet before pulling the printed document from where I hid it inside an old lesson plan binder. The altered date stares back at me, ink darker where it shouldn't be, like a bruise that never faded.

"They're watching," Eric says quietly.

"I know." I wonder how much he feels.

The words don't scare me the way they should. What scares me is how calm I feel saying them.

We sit at the kitchen table long after midnight, the park across the road nothing but a black mass against the sky. The cicadas are loud tonight—too loud, like they're trying to fill space that shouldn't be empty.

"I can stop," I say finally. I need to say it, even if I don't believe it. "I can let this go."

Eric looks at me for a long moment. "Would that actually make it stop?"

"No," I admit. "It would just teach it what works."

He exhales slowly. "Okay. Then we change how you do this."

That's how it begins. Not with a plan. With an agreement.

The next afternoon, I walk across to the park alone but don't go inside. I stand and watch people come and go—families, joggers, an older black man in a green uniform loading tools into the back of a truck. Maintenance.

I wait until he's done and walking back, ready to leave, before approaching him.

"Excuse me," I call, forcing my voice steady. "Do you work here?"

He glances back, cautious but polite. "Yeah."

"I'm a history teacher," I say. "I'm doing some research on early settlements in the area."

That word—*settlements*—lands differently here. I can feel it.

He studies me, eyes narrowing slightly. "You talking about the fort?"

"Yes," I say. Then, carefully, "And Angola."

His gaze flicks toward the trees, then back to me. "That's not something most folks ask about. Especially white folk."

"I know."

We stand there in a silence thick with evaluation. The man is deciding whether I'm dangerous—or whether pretending I don't exist is safer.

Finally, he jerks his chin toward the edge of the lot. "You want to talk, we don't do it here."

We walk to a bench half-hidden by palmettos. He sits heavily, elbows on his knees.

"I'm Simon. My grandmother used to tell stories," he says without looking at me. "Not the kind you find in books."

My pulse picks up.

"She said people ran through here. At night. Said the water carried them south."

The words hit me like a physical blow.

"The Saltwater Railroad," I whisper.

His head snaps up. "You know that name?"

I nod. "I didn't. Not before."

He lets out a short, humorless laugh. "My grandmother called it the boat path. Said the stars told you where to go."

I pull my notebook from my bag, hesitating. "Did your grandmother ever mention names?"

He goes still. After a long moment, he says, "Eli."

The sound of it rings through me. Not like a voice. Like recognition.

I write it down with shaking fingers. The moment the pen lifts from the page, the air shifts. Subtle. Focused. Pressure blooms behind my eyes.

Eli.

The name presses itself into me, heavy with sorrow and warmth and a face I don't fully see, and my breath stutters.

"You okay?" the man asks.

"Yes," I lie. "Just—thank you."

That night, the name comes again.

I'm washing dishes when it settles into my thoughts, unmistakable and deliberate, not imagined, not guessed.

Eli.

I say it aloud, and the glass in my hand fractures cleanly in two.

I gasp as the pieces fall into the sink, my heart racing. Water spills over the counter, soaking my sleeves.

Eric is there instantly. "What happened?"

"A name," I say, breathless. "It gave me a name."

He doesn't laugh. He doesn't ask what I mean. He grabs a towel and starts mopping up water with practiced calm.

"Write it down," he says. "Before you forget."

I do. Relieved. Eric is now an ally I can trust. Someone I can lean on.

The next name comes the following morning.

Ruth.

This one arrives while I'm stopped at a red light near the park.

The word settles into my chest as a stone dropped into deep water. My eyes sting, tears blurring the road ahead.

I pull over and write it down with hands that won't stop shaking.

By the end of the week, I will have four names.

Each one comes with fragments—hands clasped in prayer, a child lifted onto a boat, the smell of wet rope and fear. None of them come with dates. None of them appear in the records.

At school, the pressure tightens.

An email from the administration suggests my curriculum be "realigned." A request to access county archives is "misplaced." The historian's name appears again—this time cc'd on a message about "community sensitivities."

History is pushing back.

Eric's compliance review drags on with no explanation. His boss stops making eye contact. Meetings are rescheduled, then canceled.

"They want me distracted. Whoever they are," Eric says one night. "Afraid."

"Are you?" I ask.

He looks at me, really looks, and smiles faintly. "Terrified."

Across the road, the park waits.

I don't go back into the clearing yet. I don't need to. The past is already moving with me, pressing names into my hands whether I ask for them or not.

Whatever is guarding the past is running out of quiet ways to stop me.

And for the first time, I understand something that makes my blood run cold and steady all at once.

The Saltwater Railroad didn't survive because it was hidden. It survived because people trusted each other enough to speak names aloud.

And I am no longer alone in listening.

Chapter Sixteen

April, When the Lie Learned to Travel

The woman comes to my classroom after the final bell, when the hallway noise thins to echoes and the custodians start their slow circuits. She stands in the doorway longer than necessary, one hand resting on the frame as if she's bracing herself.

"You left a message at my church," she says. "About a name."

I nod, inviting her in, and close the door behind her.

We sit across from each other at student desks. She introduces herself as **Maribel Freeman**, voice steady but eyes watchful. I slide my notebook toward her, careful with the pages now, like they might cut.

"I'm looking for people who recognize these," I say, and tap the list. "Family stories. Anything that didn't make it into records."

She doesn't read the whole page. Her gaze goes straight to one name.

Eli.

Her breath catches. "My great-great-grandfather," she says.

"My grandmother called him *the one who watched the water*."

The room seems to lean closer. Something is watching. Listening.

Maribel reaches into her purse and takes out a folded scrap of paper, yellowed and soft at the creases. "She said it wasn't a prayer," she tells me. "It was directions."

She unfolds it carefully. The handwriting is cramped and slanted, ink faded but deliberate.

Follow the black water south.

Go when the moon breaks on the surface.

Trust the salt.

Do not stop when the land ends.

"The Saltwater Railroad," I whisper.

Maribel nods. "They didn't all make it. But some did. Cuba. The Bahamas. She said British wreckers found them—half-starved, desperate—and took them on. Said the boats came out of nowhere, like the sea was helping."

My chest tightens with something that feels like recognition and grief braided together.

"There was a raid," she adds quietly. "That's what scattered everyone. That's when the names went quiet."

The word *raid* follows me home like a shadow.

That night, when the house settles and Eric sleeps, the past opens without asking.

April.

The end of the month brings orders dressed up as opportunity. Men with money and influence decide that human lives can be had cheaply if you know where to look. They hire chiefs and promise a reward. They gather a war party—two hundred Cowetas, armed and instructed to move down the western coast of Florida, southerly.

The order is simple: take everyone with dark skin you can find. Men. Women. Children. Secure them. Deliver them to a place that will not be named.

The lie learns to travel that way—quiet, official, carried on the backs of others.

They come fast.

Angola wakes to shouting and smoke, to the crack of rifles and the thud of boots. Plantations are stripped bare. Houses burn until the air itself tastes of ash. Three hundred are taken, roped, marched, and vanish into a line of fear moving north.

I run with my mother until the ground shakes beneath us. I watch neighbors fall. I hear names screamed and cut off.

The raiders don't stop at Angola. They push south, surprising settlements, snatching more lives, until they reach the Spanish ranches near the bay.

When they find fewer people than promised, they take property instead—nets, boats, tools, anything that can be carried. Excess follows like a shadow. It always does.

When they turn back toward Georgia, the prisoners go with them. Most are never seen again.

After, the land is chaos.

Families scatter into swamps and hammocks. Seminoles vanish deeper into the Everglades. Red Stick Creeks break apart and run.

Some give up on land altogether. Canoes slip into the night, carrying those who are tired of waiting for mercy from paper and ink.

Three hundred leave by water—down through the Keys, then out into open sea. British wrecking vessels take them on where they can. Saltwater becomes a road because land has failed.

The Saltwater Railroad runs hardest when the terror is freshest.

I stay. I stay because my mother cannot move fast enough. I stay because someone must remember which way the boats went when the fires were still burning behind them.

I wake with the echo of oars in my arms.

Eric is already awake, sitting beside me. "You said a date," he tells me gently. "And 'April.'"

I swallow. "The raiders came in April."

The next day at school, the pushback sharpens.

A meeting request from administration lands in my inbox—*urgent*. The county historian's name is cc'd again, this time alongside a note about "community relationships" and "sensitive material." The tone is polite. The message is not.

History is trying to close ranks. I don't cancel my plans.

That afternoon, I met Maribel again—this time in the park parking lot, away from buildings and paper trails. She brings her aunt, who brings another story. A maintenance worker wanders close enough to listen without being seen.

Names surface like stones breaking water.

Eli.

Ruth.

Samuel.

Each one lands with weight. With images. With direction.

Eric's phone buzzes while we're driving home.

Another delay. Another review. Another soft threat wrapped in a process.

"They're tightening," he says.

I look across the road at the dark line of trees and understand, with sudden clarity, that this is the moment the story stops being private.

"They did this before," I say. "They scattered people so no one could speak together."

Eric nods once. "Then we don't let them."

That night, the presence returns—but not the cold one. The patient one.

My name was Josiah; it presses into me, finally, gently. *I stayed to watch the way out.*

I sit with the name until it settles.

The lie learned to travel in April.

But so did the truth.

And this time, the road runs through people who are willing to say the names out loud.

Chapter Seventeen

What They Call Sensitive

The meeting is scheduled for eight-thirty, which tells me everything I need to know.

Early enough that no students will be around. Early enough that whatever happens can be contained, summarized, and filed away before anyone has time to ask questions. I dressed carefully that morning—not professionally, but deliberately. Comfortable shoes. No jewelry that might jingle if my hands shake.

Eric watches from the doorway as I gather my bag.

"You don't have to go alone," he says.

"I do," I answer. "But I won't be unprepared."

He nods, jaw tight. "I'll be close."

The conference room smells like coffee and printer toner. Three administrators sit along one side of the table. The county historian, Harold Miller, sits at the end, hands folded, expression neutral enough to pass for kind.

"Thank you for coming, Ms. Rivera," the principal says. "This won't take long." That, too, is a lie.

They talk first. They always do. About curriculum alignment. About parent concerns that haven't yet materialized but might.

About the importance of teaching history "responsibly." I let them finish.

"Which part is irresponsible?" I ask.

A pause. The historian clears his throat. "Angola is… complicated," he says. "The documentation is incomplete. Presenting contested narratives can confuse students."

"Incomplete because it was altered," I say calmly. "Contested because it was erased."

The principal's smile tightens. "This isn't about debate. It's about suitability."

"Suitability for whom?" I ask, trying not to raise my voice.

No one answers that.

I slide copies of the altered document onto the table—just one page, nothing inflammatory at first glance. Dates. Margins. Ink.

The historian doesn't touch it.

"This document hasn't been verified," he says.

"Neither have the versions you're comfortable with," I reply.

The silence that follows is thick, institutional. I recognize it now. This is how power sounds when it believes it is being patient.

"We're asking you to pause this line of inquiry," the principal says. "For now."

There it is.

"I can't," I say.

The historian finally looks me directly in the eye. His eyes are not cruel. That's what makes him dangerous.

"You're risking more than your job," he says quietly. "Some histories don't stay academic."

It's a veiled threat.

I think of Eric's stalled car. The compliance review. The way the park goes quiet when I get too close to the truth.

"I know," I say.

When the meeting ends, nothing is resolved. That's deliberate too. Uncertainty is a tool. It keeps you awake at night. It makes you doubt yourself. I don't doubt myself anymore.

That afternoon, I didn't go home right away. I drive past the park and keep going, toward a small church I found through Maribel. No sign out front. No website. Just a gravel lot and a building that's been repaired more times than it's been renovated. Inside, a handful of people wait.

Not a meeting. Not officially. Just people who have heard a name and recognized it as their own.

We sit in a loose circle. No one records anything. Phones stay in pockets. Stories come slowly at first, then faster—like water finding a channel.

"My great-aunt said they went by canoe."

"My family said they followed the stars."

"They never talked about Georgia. Just water."

An older woman raises her cane, and everyone stops to listen.

"I'm Etta Barlow. My grandmother told me stories, but never said *Angola*.

She said *that place by the water*.

When I was little, I thought she meant anywhere with a river.

We lived near one then, brown and slow, nothing like the springs I would see decades later. I didn't understand why my grandmother's voice changed whenever we passed it—why she tightened her grip on my hand, why she rushed us home before dusk.

"Don't linger near water at night," she used to say.

Not afraid. Certain.

I thought it was superstition. Old people always have rules that don't come with explanations.

It wasn't until I was grown that I realized it wasn't superstition at all. It was an instruction.

My grandmother had rules for stories, too. Some you told freely. Some you told only indoors. Some you didn't tell at all.

"If you remember too loud," she warned once, "someone will hear."

I asked who.

She didn't answer.

She was born long after the raid, but the raid lived in her bones anyway. It lived in the way she packed a bag, even for short trips.

In the way she memorized routes without looking at maps. In the way, she never trusted papers more than people.

"Names matter," she told me. "But you got to know when to carry them quiet."

That part confused me the most.

Why carry something you weren't allowed to speak?

Now I know.

Silence wasn't emptiness. It was a shelter.

My grandmother learned early that survival didn't always look like defiance. Sometimes it looked like passing warnings wrapped in ordinary advice. Like telling a child not to swim too far. Like insisting doors be locked even in daylight. Like teaching us how to recognize stars we were never supposed to need.

She taught me which ones pointed south. Not directly. Never directly.

Just, "That one don't move much. You can trust it."

I didn't understand until I was old enough to understand why she cried the first time I told her I wanted to study history.

"They don't write it right," she said. "And when they do, they leave out the part where we lived."

I promised her I'd be careful.

She smiled then, tired but proud. "Be careful, yes. But don't be quiet forever."

When the woman across from the park started asking questions—when the names began to surface—I felt something in my chest loosen that I hadn't known was tight. It felt dangerous at first, like stepping into open light after a lifetime indoors.
I heard my grandmother's voice clear as day.

This is the part where you speak.

So I came.

I stood with the others by the fence and listened as names were read aloud without fear of consequence. I felt the ground hold steady beneath my feet, and for the first time, the water didn't feel like something to avoid.

It felt like a witness.

When I left that evening, I touched the earth the way my grandmother used to—flat palm, quiet respect.

"I didn't forget," I told her, though she was long gone.

The warnings did what they were meant to do.

They kept us alive long enough to return.

And now, finally, we are allowed to say why."

No one spoke for several minutes. Breaths were held.

I write nothing down. I don't need to. The names settle into me anyway.

That night, when I finally step into the park again, Josiah is already there—not visible, not solid, but present in the way a held breath is present.

"They're pushing back," I say softly.

They always do, he answers.

"Then we're running out of quiet options."

The air shifts. Agreement. Resolve.

The Saltwater Railroad only worked when people moved together, Josiah reminds me. *One boat alone is easy to stop.*

Across the road, Eric waits on the porch steps, watching.

I understand now what the choice really is. Not whether to tell the truth. But whether to let it be small enough to disappear.

I turn back toward the road, toward the lights, toward the people who are starting to gather, whether permission has been given or not.

"They can't erase us all," I say.

The land hums beneath my feet—not with warning this time, but with something that feels like momentum.

And somewhere, deep in the systems that have protected the lie for generations, something tightens—aware now that silence is no longer holding.

Chapter Eighteen

Pressure Points

The first sign that it's gone public is the email.

It arrives just after dawn, flagged *urgent*, forwarded to every social studies teacher in the district. The subject line is bland enough to pass unnoticed—*Curriculum Clarification*—but my name sits in the second paragraph like a pin pressed deliberately into place.

Recent inquiries into sensitive regional histories have raised concerns about the balance of instruction...

Eric reads it over my shoulder, jaw tightening. "They didn't have to name you."

"They wanted to," I say. "This way it looks procedural."

By the time I reach school, the hallway feels different. Not hostile—worse. Careful. Doors close a little faster. Conversations stop when I pass. The historian's influence moves like humidity: invisible, everywhere.

In the third period, the fire alarm goes off. Not a drill. The sharp, urgent kind that snaps nerves tight. Students pour into the hallway, voices overlapping. I herd them outside, my pulse steady despite the chaos.

Only when we're lined up on the field do I realize something is wrong. The alarm isn't coming from the building. It's coming from the park.

Sirens wail across the road. Police and fire department trucks cluster near the entrance, radios crackling. A maintenance truck blocks the path I took just days ago. Yellow tape goes up fast, slicing the morning into clean boundaries.

Eric texts me.

Eric: *They closed the park. "Environmental hazard." No details.*

I stare at the tape fluttering in the breeze. Environmental hazard. Renovation. Safety review. The language changes, but the goal doesn't.

Contain. Delay. Forget.

That afternoon, the principal called me back in. "We're placing you on temporary administrative leave," she says, not unkindly. "Just until things settle."

"Things like truth?" I ask.

She flinches. "This isn't personal."

It never is.

Before I leave the school grounds, a student in my class stops me.

"Ms. Rivira, you have been talking about the history and where we come from."

"Yes, I have."

"I picked my grandmother because she lives with us and because she always complains nobody asks her anything meaningful anymore.

She laughed when I told her what I needed. "You sure you want to open that drawer?"

I thought she was joking.

She wasn't.

She went quiet in that way adults do when they're deciding whether you're old enough for the truth. Then she reached into the hall closet and pulled down a shoebox I'd never seen before. Inside were papers that didn't match. Different handwriting. Different ink. Some torn. Some folded until the creases almost split. Names written in the margins. Dates with question marks beside them.

"This was your great-great," she said, tapping one page. "Or maybe great-great-great. We stopped counting cleanly at some point."

I leaned closer.

The name felt strange in my mouth when I said it out loud, like it didn't belong in history class. Like it belonged to me."

"Why didn't we know this?" I asked.

She smiled, but it didn't reach her eyes. "We did know. We just didn't say."

She told me about warnings passed down like bedtime rules. Don't linger near certain places. Don't write everything down. Don't trust maps more than people. And always—always—know which way south is.

I thought of the park. Of the names being read. Of you, Ms. Rivera, standing at the microphone with papers shaking in her hands.

"Angola," I said, testing the word.

My grandmother closed her eyes. "Yes."

The room felt different after that. Smaller. Bigger. Like the walls had shifted to make room for something that had always been there.

When I went online later, I didn't scroll the way I usually do. I searched. I cross-checked. I found pieces that lined up with the shoebox papers, as if they'd been waiting for each other.

That's when it hit me.

This wasn't just history.

This was an inheritance.

At the next gathering by the park, I didn't know where to stand at first. Everyone looked older, like they belonged in the story more than I did.

Then someone started reading names.

And I heard it.

Not my name—but close enough that my chest tightened anyway. Close enough that I knew, without needing proof, that this wasn't a coincidence.

When it was my turn to speak, my voice shook.

"I didn't know," I said. "But I do now."

Nobody laughed. Nobody corrected me.

Someone nodded like that was enough.

On the way home, my phone buzzed with messages from friends asking what it felt like to find out something that big. I didn't know how to answer yet.

All I knew was this: I wasn't just learning history.

History had reached forward and tapped me on the shoulder and said, *You're part of this now."*

My student has tears in her eyes. I do too. I reach out, hug her close, and feel her grandmother's words embracing me.

At home, Eric paces while I sit at the table, notebook open, names written in careful rows. Eli. Ruth. Samuel. More now—six, then eight, then ten—each arriving with a sense of urgency I can feel in my bones.

"They're trying to scare us," Eric says.

"They're trying to isolate us," I correct. "That's how it worked before."

As if summoned by the thought, the air in the room tightens. Not grief. Not memory. Authority.

The lights flicker. Eric freezes.

"Gabby," he says quietly. "Tell me this isn't what I think it is."

Before I can answer, the pressure shifts—sharp, targeted. The sound of the house creaking isn't natural this time. It's forced, like something testing limits.

Then Josiah presses in—fast, urgent, burning through the space like a warning flare.

It's reaching for him, he says. *Not you.*

The realization hits hard and clean.

"Eric," I say, standing. "Get your keys."

"What?"

"Now."

We leave the house just as the power cuts out completely. The porch light snaps off. The silence that follows is absolute.

Across the road, beyond the tape and the trucks and the official explanations, the land hums with restrained fury.

In the dark, I understand something crucial.

This thing—the hostile presence—it can't hurt me directly. But it can hurt everything I love.

Eric grips the steering wheel, knuckles white. "How far does this go?"

I think of April. Of orders dressed as opportunity. Of boats slipping into water because land had become a trap.

"As far as we let it," I say.

The names in my notebook feel heavier now, not just memory but obligation.

Behind us, the house stands dark and quiet, just another structure on a road pretending it hasn't been built over bones.

Ahead of us, people are already talking, already noticing, already asking why the park is closed and why a history teacher has been sidelined for asking questions.

The lie has moved into daylight.

And daylight is where it starts to crack.

Chapter Nineteen

How Silence Learned to Survive

I did not stay because I was brave.

That is the lie people like to tell afterward, when they need meaning to sit neatly where horror once lived. Courage makes a better story than fear. So does sacrifice.

The truth is more straightforward. I stayed because silence arrived before I could leave.

After the raid, after the fires burned themselves into memory, after the canoes slipped south carrying those who still believed water might be kinder than land, something settled over Angola that had never been there before.

Not quiet.

Control.

Men came after the smoke cleared. Not soldiers this time. Clerks. Surveyors. People who carried paper instead of guns. They walked the ground with measured steps, careful not to look too closely at what lay beneath.

They asked questions that were already answered.

"How many?"

"Where did they go?"

"Are you certain?"

Each question shaved the truth smaller.

They did not record the screams. They did not record the way children clung to skirts or the sound a body makes when it is dragged across sand. They recorded *movements. Dispersals. Incidents.* They didn't count the dead.

They wrote as if no one had decided anything.

I watched from the trees as they spoke to those who remained. To the frightened. To the hungry. To the ones who had not yet learned that survival sometimes requires agreeing with the person holding the pen.

"You're safe now," they said.

"This is for your protection."

"It's better not to stir things up."

That was how silence learned its first trick.

It made itself sound like mercy.

Those who argued disappeared into paperwork. Those who asked too many questions were labeled unreliable. Dangerous. Emotional. The land was surveyed and renamed. The paths we ran were marked as trails, then erased altogether.

And the people who stayed—those too old to flee, too broken to move, too attached to graves that no longer had markers—learned what happened when they spoke.

They learned that memory could cost you food. Shelter. Safety. They learned that silence was cheaper.

I watched a woman—no older than Gabby is now—press her mouth shut with her hand when a clerk asked if she'd seen anyone taken north. Her eyes flicked to her child. Then to the man with the ledger.

"No," she said.

The lie slid into place as easily as breath.

That was the moment I understood.

The hostile presence did not begin with violence. Violence was only the opening argument. What followed was refinement. Process. The quiet repetition of authority until resistance felt pointless.

Silence survived because it adapted.

It learned to wear the language of order. Of protection. Of professionalism.

It learned to wait.

Years passed. Roads were cut through the land. Houses rose and fell. The springs were named and renamed. Angola became a rumor, then a footnote, then nothing at all.

I tried to speak once.

Not with words—I no longer had those—but with weight. With cold. With the way the air tightens before a storm. A man digging near the water froze, shovel mid-air, and whispered, "Did you hear that?"

He ran.

The next day, a sign went up warning of unstable ground.

They called it natural.

That was the second lesson silence taught me.

When truth presses back, rename it.

I learned restraint after that. Learned to stay folded into the land, to let memory settle instead of surge. I listened as generations passed stories in fragments—directions without explanations, prayers that sounded like nonsense until you knew what they hid.

Follow the black water.

Trust the salt.

Do not stop when land ends.

That was how the Saltwater Railroad survived.

Not openly. Not safely. But enough.

When Gabby arrived, when she paused instead of passing through, I felt the old balance tilt. Silence recognized her, too. It always recognizes threats before it names them.

That is why it moved so quickly through institutions, through meetings, emails, and warnings wrapped in concern. It remembered what worked.

But silence has a weakness it never learned to correct. It depends on people believing they are alone.

I stayed because someone had to remember how the lie was built.

Not the fire. Not the guns.

The paperwork.

The pauses.

The moment when fear made agreement feel like safety.

When Gabby speaks the names aloud—when she brings others together so no one carries the truth alone—the structure that has protected silence for two centuries will fracture because silence does not survive witnesses.

And this time, there are too many listeners.

Chapter Twenty

What Surfaces When Water Is Lowered

The park closure lasts three days.

That's how long it takes before the questions stop sounding polite. Three days before, joggers complained, before parents ask why their children's favorite trail is suddenly off-limits. Before fishermen notice access points roped off with no explanation, that stays consistent longer than a single news cycle.

Eric tracks it all from the kitchen table, laptop open, news tabs multiplying.

"They're calling it an environmental review now," he says.

"Yesterday, it was a sinkhole risk. This morning it's 'routine maintenance.'"

I sit across from him, notebook open, pen resting in the crease of my palm. The names feel heavier today, as if they know something I don't yet.

"Silence is improvising," I say.

Eric looks up. "That good or bad?"

"It means we're forcing it to adapt."

On the fourth morning, the water level at the springs drops. Not dramatically. Not enough to trigger alarms. Just enough.

The limestone shelf near the old clearing emerges where it usually stays hidden—dark rock slick with algae, threaded with debris that hasn't seen daylight in generations. Something old catches there, wedged where the current once hid it.

Wood. Not driftwood. Worked wood. A plank edge smoothed by water but still square. A joint that shouldn't exist if nothing had ever been built—or broken—here.

My chest tightens. I feel Josiah before I hear him. Not as words. As gravity.

This is where it ended, he presses into me. *For me.*

Maribel texts first.

Maribel: *Something's showing near the south trail. Rangers are pretending it's nothing. It isn't.*

I don't answer right away.

Eric looks at me and sighs. "We're going."

"We're not sneaking," I say. "We're being seen." That matters now.

We don't cross the tape. We don't need to. People have already gathered—locals, a few park staff who are suddenly very invested in their phones, two reporters pretending they're just out for a walk.

The limestone shelf is visible from where we stand.

So is the wood.

Someone gasps softly.

A worker clears his throat. "That's just debris," he says, too fast. "Old dock material."

"From where?" I ask.

He shrugs but doesn't answer.

The air tightens—not with grief this time, but with attention. Phones rise, the Cameras focus. Silence does not retreat. It braces.

I kneel near the edge of the tape, ignoring the warning signs. The ground hums faintly beneath my palm—cooler now, closer.

And then the past breaks open.

The attack comes before dawn.

I am running toward the water, not away from it, because the north is fire and shouting and the crack of rifles splitting the air. I hear my mother behind me, breath ragged, calling my name.

"Josiah!" I turn back. That is the mistake.

A shot cracks—sharp, close. Pain explodes through my side, knocking the breath from my lungs. I stumble into the sand, hands sinking deep as if the earth is trying to hold me. I taste iron.

The boats are right there. Canoes half-pushed into the water. People are scrambling, crying, shoving off before the raiders reach the shoreline. Someone grabs my arm, tries to pull me up.

"I can't," I choke.

My mother drops to her knees beside me. Her hands are shaking, slick with blood as she presses them against my wound.

"I won't leave you," she says.

I know she will die if she stays.

"Go," I tell her. She shakes her head, sobbing, and that is when I do the only thing I can.

I push her. Hard.

She falls backward into the arms of another woman, and the canoe lurches as they scramble aboard. I shout her name once— just once—before the pain takes my voice.

The last thing I see is her face as the boat pulls away, her mouth open in a scream, the water swallows her whole.

Boots pound the sand.

A shadow falls over me.

I don't feel the second shot.

The water laps closer, gentle, persistent. It reaches my fingers, then my palm. The sky lightens, indifferent.

I stay because I have nowhere left to go.

I gasp and jerk back, breath tearing from my lungs. Eric's hand closes around my shoulder. "Gabby."

The limestone shelf blurs through tears I didn't feel start.

"That's where he died," I whisper. "He was shot trying to get others onto the boats."

The county truck pulls up too fast. The historian, Harold Miller, steps out, jacket immaculate, gaze sharp.

"This area is unstable," he announces. "Please clear the perimeter."

"No," Maribel says calmly, her hands on her hips, defiant. The word lands like a stone dropped into still water.

"My family ran from here," she continues. "You don't get to call it unstable and expect us to move."

Murmurs ripple outward.
The historian turns toward me. "Ms. Rivera. You've done enough."

I stand. "No," I say. "I've finally done enough to be honest." I take out my notebook.

I don't read all the names. Not yet. I choose one. "Josiah," I say, the ground hums.

"He stayed so others could leave," I continue. "He died here. And he stayed here because no one wrote that down."

A woman in the crowd makes a broken sound. Maribel grips her arm.

"My grandmother said he watched the water," she whispers.

"Yes," I say. "He did."

The historian looks at the exposed wood again, at the limestone shelf, at the people filming now without apology.

For the first time, he looks uncertain.

Eric's phone buzzes—alerts stacking, messages spreading faster than silence can contain.

"They're sharing this," he murmurs. "All of it."

Good.

Because silence learned to survive by isolating pain, and truth survives by being spoken together.

I feel Josiah close—not heavy, not bound, just present.

This is enough, he tells me, *for now.*

Across the water, the birds begin to sing again—hesitant at first, then louder.

And for the first time since April of 1821, the place where Josiah fell is no longer quiet.

Eric drives with me to school the next day. The first thing that disappears is my access badge. I don't notice it until I try to enter the faculty lot, and the gate doesn't lift. I swipe again. The red light blinks, impersonal and final.

A security guard I barely know approaches, apologetic but firm.

"You'll need to park in the visitor lot today, Ms. Rivera."

"Why?"

He hesitates. "Administrative directive."

That phrase again. Authority without ownership.

Inside, the hallway feels colder. Not hostile — *withdrawn.*

Conversations dip as I pass. Eyes slide away. Silence is learning to move faster now. I make it to my classroom before the email hits.

Subject: *Temporary Suspension Pending Review*

Eric reads it over my shoulder, hand settling at my back. "They're trying to freeze you out."

"They're trying to make me disappear," I say.

Eric kisses my forehead and leaves for work. He's worried but tries not to show it.

I carry on with my day.

By the third period, a reporter is waiting in the parking lot.

Eric is there to meet me at the school door and shields me from the reporter. He hustles me to the car.

I don't speak to Eric—not yet—but the fact that the reporter is there tells me something important: the containment failed. Someone shared footage. Someone shared names.

Silence is bleeding.

On the way home, Eric's phone rings. He listens, expression tightening with each word, until he finally says, "We'll cooperate fully," and hangs up.

"They pulled me into a formal investigation," he says quietly.

"Financial compliance. Ethics review."

"For what?" I demand.

He shakes his head. "They didn't say. That's the point."

I feel Josiah stir — not urgently, not warning — *resentful.* *This is how they punish witnesses,* he presses into me. *Sideways.*

We don't go home right away. Instead, we drive the long way, circling the park without stopping. Police tape still flutters at the south trail. A county truck idles nearby, engine running even though no one is inside.

"They're afraid of the land now," Eric says.

"They should be."

That night, someone left a note on our door.

No name. No threat. Just four words, written neatly on unlined paper:

LET THE DEAD REST

Eric crumples it in his fist. "They don't get to decide that."

I don't sleep.

Instead, I spread my notebooks across the kitchen table —
names, dates, fragments, maps. I stop trying to make them orderly.

Order is what silence uses.

I start grouping instead.

Families. Routes. Escape points. Patterns emerge that were
never meant to be seen together.

This is it, Josiah tells me quietly, *the moment they cannot undo.*

The next morning, I sent three emails.

One to Maribel.

One to the reporters who have been circling.

One to the school board.

Subject: *Public History Presentation – Angola*

Eric watches me hit send. "This ends quietly or loudly," he
says.

I meet his eyes. "It never ends quietly."

Outside, the birds fall silent — not in fear, not in warning —
but in anticipation.

Silence has survived for two hundred years by convincing
people they are alone.

It won't survive what comes next.

Chapter Twenty-One

How Silence Learns to Breathe

Silence does not shout.

If it did, it would be easy to recognize. Easy to resist. Instead, it learns how to sound reasonable.

After the raids, after the bodies were buried without markers and the boats vanished into water that promised distance but not safety, silence took a new shape.

It learned to arrive with a clipboard. With a meeting time. With a careful smile that suggested cooperation was the same thing as peace.

People who spoke were not punished loudly.

They were delayed. Many are taken North back to slavery. Returned to the owners whom they had run from.

Their requests are misplaced. Their credibility is questioned. Their livelihoods were quietly complicated until survival demanded attention elsewhere. Silence learned that hunger and fear work better than force.

It learned that paperwork lasts longer than gunfire. The land remembered anyway.

That was the problem.

So silence adapted again. It allowed the land to be renamed. Surveyed. Measured. Converted into something recreational, something managed. A park. A destination. A place where history could be reduced to plaques that did not say enough to disturb anyone.

What could not be erased was softened.

What could not be softened was fragmented.

One story here. Another there. No names spoken together. No witnesses allowed to recognize each other across time.

Silence survives by keeping memory lonely.

That is why it reacts so violently now.

Not because the past is returning — the past never left — but because the living have begun to gather it into one place. One voice becoming many. One name answered by another.

Silence can endure grief.

It cannot endure a chorus.

Chapter Twenty-Two

When the Doors Open

The announcement doesn't come from me. That's how I know we've crossed a line.

It breaks midmorning, threaded through group texts and local feeds before any official statement has time to catch up. Someone posts a short clip from the springs—water lowered, wood exposed, my voice saying *Eli Freeman*—and tags it with a question that spreads faster than answers ever do:

Why was this never taught?

By noon, the school board's website crashes.

Eric reads updates aloud from the couch, phone glowing in his hand. "Community forum. Emergency session. Open comment."

I sit at the table with my notebook closed for once. The names are already out there. I don't need to push them anymore. They're moving on their own.

"They're calling it a listening session," he adds.

I laugh, a short sound that surprises us both. "They always do."

The hostile presence tightens—not like before, not with quiet threats, but with friction. The house creaks. The air presses in on us. Emails land in my inbox with subject lines that carry the sheen of neutrality: *Clarification Requested. Opportunity to Reframe. Concerned Stakeholders.*

Silence is changing tactics.

A knock at the door cuts through the noise.

Two people stand on the porch: a woman with a clipboard and a man in a county jacket. Polite. Professional. Apologetic in advance.

"We just want to ask a few questions," the woman says. "Off the record."

"No," Eric says, stepping forward before I can speak. He slams the door shut. The word hangs there, complete and straightforward.

They leave without arguing. Silence doesn't argue when it's losing. It documents.

By late afternoon, the forum details are everywhere. Location: the high school auditorium. Time: seven p.m. *All are welcome. All,* Josiah presses into me gently. *That is the part they cannot control.*

At six-thirty, the parking lot is already full.

I recognize faces as we walk in—Maribel, the groundskeeper, a county worker who wouldn't meet my eyes before, and does now. People I've never seen nod at me like we share something unspoken.

Eric squeezes my hand. "Whatever happens," he says, "we don't split up."

Inside, the air hums with voices layered over each other, the sound of people bracing for disagreement. A banner reads **"Community Listening Session"** in a friendly font.

Silence dressed for daylight.

The board sits onstage behind a long table. The historian, Mr. Miller, is there too, composed, hands folded. Cameras dot the back wall. Someone is live-streaming.

When public comment opens, the first speaker surprises everyone.

An elderly black man steps to the microphone, hands shaking, voice steady. "My grandmother ran from Angola," he says. "I didn't know the name until last week. I know it now."

Applause ripples, tentative at first, then stronger.

A woman follows. "My grandmother told us not to ask questions. She said asking made things worse."

Another voice: "Why were the dates changed?"

Another: "Why didn't we learn this?"

Silence tries to respond with process.

"We need verified sources—"

"This is complicated—"

"We must be careful—"

Each phrase lands weaker than the one before.

When my name is called, the room stills.

I walk to the microphone without my notebook. I don't need it.

"This isn't about blame," I say. "It's about acknowledgment. Angola wasn't erased by accident. It was erased by design."

The historian shifts. The lights flicker once, sharp and brief.

Eric stiffens in his seat beside the aisle.

I feel the pressure then—focused, desperate.

It will reach for him again, Josiah warns. *Stand.*

"I'm not asking permission," I continue. "I'm asking for participation. Names matter because people matter. And when we speak them together, they stop being easy to dismiss."

I say three names: Eli, Ruth, and Samuel. The room answers me. Recognition. Tears. Murmurs of *that was my family.*

Silence pulls hard—emails sent in real time, calls made, favors invoked—but it's too late. Witness has mass now.

A reporter shouts a question. Someone else starts chanting, "Say the names—soft at first, then louder."

The board chair bangs a gavel that no one hears.

Eric's phone buzzes. He looks at it, then at me, eyes wide.

"They dropped the review," he whispers. "Effective immediately."

Relief surges—and then something colder slides in behind it.

The lights dim again. Not flicker. Dim.

A hum builds in the walls, the sound of systems straining. *This is the last push,* Josiah says. *Hold.*

I grip the edge of the podium, steadying myself. The chant swells, carrying me, carrying us.

Silence has one final move left.

And it's about to spend it in public.

Chapter Twenty-Three

What Breaks in the Open

The lights don't go out. They *hesitate*.

That's the detail that will matter later, when people argue about what happened next. Not a blackout. Not sabotage. A pause long enough for everyone to notice, short sufficient to deny intent.

The hum in the walls deepens, vibrating through the seats, the microphones, the metal legs of the folding chairs. A few people laugh nervously. Someone near the back swears.

"Please remain calm," the board chair says, voice cracking through the speakers.

Silence presses hard—focused, furious now. I feel it searching for leverage, the way a hand searches a wall for a light switch. *It's looking for a single point,* Josiah warns. *Something it can collapse.*

A screen behind the board flickers to life without being cued. Not slides. Not an agenda. An email thread.

My name is there, bolded in a subject line. Then Eric's. Then a cascade of timestamps, compliance language, and phrases clipped from context, stacked to suggest wrongdoing without ever stating it outright.

A collective inhale ripples through the room.

"This—" the historian begins, rising from his seat. "This is inappropriate—"

"Is it?" someone calls out.

The screen scrolls on its own. Another document appears. A memo stamped **DRAFT**. A sentence highlighted in yellow: *Potential reputational risk.*

Silence is doing what it has always done best—burying truth under implication.

Eric stands. He doesn't rush the stage. He doesn't shout. He turns to face the room, shoulders squared, hands visible.

"That review was dropped," he says clearly. "You heard that already. What you're seeing now is an attempt to scare us back into quiet."

A murmur spreads—agreement, recognition. Phones lift higher. Someone zooms in, capturing the drafts, the timestamps, the tells that anyone who's worked inside systems recognizes instantly.

I step forward again. "This is what erasure looks like in real time," I say. "Not denial. *Distraction.*"

The lights brighten—too bright—then settle. The hum wavers. Silence tightens, desperate. It pushes once more, hard enough that my vision blurs. I taste iron, the room tilts.

Now, Josiah says. *Say it now.*

I close my eyes—not to retreat, but to listen.

I speak the names. Not three this time. More. A rhythm forms as I say them, a cadence that pulls answers from the crowd.

"Here."

"My family."

"I remember."

The chant changes, becomes steadier, less angry, and more resolute. **Say the names** gives way to **We are here**.

That's when the screen goes dark. Not flicker. Not pause. Off.

The historian sinks back into his chair, pale. The board chair lowers the gavel and doesn't raise it again.

Silence tries to retreat—but it can't pull itself back together once it's been seen this clearly. Once drafts, delays, and threats have been named for what they are.

A reporter steps forward, voice cutting through the noise. "Is the board prepared to explain why these documents exist?"

Another voice: "Will the park reopen?"

Another: "Will the records be corrected?"

Questions stack faster than answers can be managed.

I feel Josiah loosen—just a little. Not gone. Not yet. But lighter.

This is enough to break the lock, he tells me. *The door will open now, even if it creaks.*

Eric reaches me, hand warm and solid around mine. "You okay?"

I nod. My knees are shaking, but I'm upright. We both are.

As the meeting dissolves into interviews and arguments and plans that can't be quietly undone, I understand the final truth about silence.

It doesn't die when confronted.

It dies when it can no longer pretend it's alone with you.

Outside, as people spill into the night still talking, still recording, still naming, the cicadas resume their song—hesitant at first, then full.

Across the road, beyond the lights and the noise, the land exhales.

And for the first time since 1821, nothing moves to stop it.

Chapter Twenty-Four

What Stays, What Lifts

The night doesn't end cleanly.

There's no moment when the doors close and everyone agrees on what just happened. People linger in the parking lot under buzzing lights, talking in low, urgent clusters. Reporters hover. Board members retreat through side exits.

Silence doesn't vanish—it thins, stretches, looks for someplace quieter to regroup.

Eric and I sit in the car with the engine off, hands still linked, neither of us ready to turn the key.

"You feel different," he says finally.

"So do you."

He nods. "Like something stepped back."

Across the road, the park is dark again, but not sealed, not braced. The air feels looser, as if the land has stopped holding itself rigid against a blow it expected and didn't quite receive.

This is the first loosening, Josiah tells me. His presence is gentler now, less anchored to the places of pain. *Not released. But relief.*

At home, exhaustion hits all at once. My body remembers it is human. I shower, watching water carry the day down the drain, and for the first time since we moved, the water smells like water—no smoke, no iron, no salt.

I sleep.

Not dreams of fire. Not boats. Just dark, unbroken rest.

Morning brings consequences. By ten a.m., the district issues a statement—carefully worded, noncommittal, promising "review" and "community collaboration." The park closure is reclassified as *temporary*. A task force is announced. Records will be "reexamined."

Eric snorts when he reads it. "They're still trying to control the narrative."

"Yes," I say. "But now they have to admit there is one."

Maribel calls before noon.

"They're organizing a public history day," she says. "At the park. They want you involved."

I close my eyes, feeling the land stir at the mention of it. "I will be."

That afternoon, I walked alone to the edge of the springs.

No tape. No trucks. Just the slow, honest sound of water moving where it always has. The limestone shelf is submerged again, but I know what rests there now—not hidden, not denied.

"I didn't forget," I say softly.

I know, Josiah answers.

The weight that has always accompanied his presence feels different—no longer pulling downward, but outward, like something preparing to let go.

"I stayed," he tells me, not as an explanation now, but as closure. *I stayed so the way would not vanish. But I don't need to hold it alone anymore.*

A breeze moves through the trees. Birds lift, startled, then settle again.

"Does that mean you're leaving, crossing over, whatever spirits do?" I ask.

A pause. Then warmth, quiet, and sure.

Not yet. Some things release slowly. But I am no longer trapped.

That night, Eric and I sit on the porch with no agenda, just listening to the ordinary sounds of evening. He leans back, eyes closed.

"I thought helping meant fixing," he says. "Turns out it just meant standing still long enough not to get pulled away."

I smile. "That's harder."

He opens his eyes. "Are you scared?"

I consider it.

"Yes," I say. "But not of this."

Across the road, the park holds its shape in the dark—no longer a mouth, no longer a warning. Just land, carrying what it carries, finally allowed to speak without being punished for it.

Some silences break all at once.

Others loosen, grain by grain.

This one has begun to lift.

And for the first time, I believe it will keep lifting—because it no longer belongs to one voice, one ghost, one waiting witness.

It belongs to all of us now.

Chapter Twenty-Five

The Cost of Truth

The first thing I learn about telling the truth in daylight is that it multiplies. Not just in support—though there is plenty of that now—but consequence. Every statement invites a response. Every correction exposes another gap. It was about uncovering what had been hidden. The next is about living with what refuses to stay buried.

By Monday morning, my inbox is unusable. It is filled with interview requests. Invitations to panels I don't trust yet. Warnings disguised as advice. One unsigned email simply says: "Be careful what you become known for."

Eric reads it over my shoulder. "They're still hoping you'll self-edit."

"I'm past that," I say, surprised at how calm I feel.

The district reinstates me with conditions.

I'm allowed back in the classroom—but not to teach anything "outside the approved framework" until the task force completes its work. It's framed as a compromise. It feels like containment.

"I'll take it," I tell the principal. "For now."

Silence shifts at that word.

For now, it is dangerous.

The park reopens in stages. County workers walk trails with clipboards and rehearsed explanations. New temporary signage goes up—careful, neutral language that acknowledges "historical significance" without naming who suffered or why.

People bring flowers anyway. They leave them near the springs, tucked into the roots of trees, weighted with stones so they won't float away. Someone leaves a laminated card with three names written in thick marker.

Eli.

Ruth.

Samuel.

More appear by the next morning.

The Miller requests a meeting. Not public. Not recorded.

"No," Eric says when I tell him.

"Yes," I reply. "But not alone."

We meet in a conference room with glass walls, transparency performative but real enough to matter. The historian looks tired now. Older. The careful neutrality he wore like armor has begun to chafe.

"You've made this… difficult," he says.

"I didn't," I answer. "The truth did."

He exhales. "You're forcing institutions to move faster than they're designed to."

"Good," I say.

For a moment, he looks at me without calculation. "Do you know how many careers depend on the way this history has been told?"

"Yes," I say. "Do you know how many lives depended on it being hidden?"

Silence stretches—not the hostile one, not anymore. This is human silence. Uncomfortable. Necessary.

"We can correct some records," he says finally. "Adjust language. Add context."

"Names," I say.

Miller flinches. "That's… complicated."

"Only if you're afraid of who recognizes themselves."

When I leave, nothing is resolved. But something has shifted again—less resistance, more fracture. Silence doesn't hold clean lines anymore. It leaks.

That night, Josiah comes to me without urgency. *They are trying to save the shape of things,* he says. *Not the truth.*

"And you?"

I am learning how to let go without disappearing.

His presence is thinner now, like mist at the edge of morning. I feel it and don't reach for it, understanding for the first time that holding on too tightly is another kind of erasure.

At school, students ask questions that aren't on the syllabus.

"Why didn't we learn this before?"

"Who decides what counts as history?"

"Does fixing the records fix what happened?"

I answer honestly.

"No."

"People."

"It's a start."

Outside the classroom, pressure builds again—but in a different way. Not sharp. Not violent. Legal. Procedural. Slow.

A state-level review is announced. Funding is mentioned. The phrase *politically sensitive* reappears, dusted off and put back to work.

Eric feels it too.

"They're not done," he says one evening, watching headlights pass on the road. "They've just changed tactics."

"I know."

Across the street, the park is busy with evening walkers, families, people who don't yet know they're crossing a threshold that history has reopened.

The birds don't fall silent anymore when I step outside.

They watch.

It's about endurance.

And I understand now what Josiah understood too late—that telling the truth doesn't end the danger. It only changes where the danger lives.

The question isn't whether silence will push back.

It's how much we're willing to lose before it finally breaks for good.

Chapter Twenty-Six

What Pushes Back Harder

The first threat comes wrapped in concern.

It arrives as a voicemail while I'm in class, the caller ID blocked, the tone careful and almost kind.

"Ms. Rivera, we strongly advise you to reconsider your involvement in upcoming public programming related to Angola. There are funding considerations you may not be aware of. Please call us back."

I don't.

By lunch, the concern sharpens.

A memo circulates warning staff against "unauthorized public statements." My name isn't on it, but everyone knows who it's for.

A colleague slips into my classroom after the bell and softly shuts the door.

"Be careful," she whispers. "They're talking about audits."

Audits. Reviews. Compliance.

The words hit harder now that I know how silence uses them.

That evening, Eric's car doesn't start.

Not stall—*won't start*. The dash lights flicker once, then die. He sits there, hands on the wheel, breathing slow, controlled.

"This isn't random," he says when I come out.

I don't argue.

Across the road, the park is full of evening walkers, laughter drifting through the trees. The normalcy makes my skin crawl.

It is reminding you, Josiah presses into me. *That it still has reach.*

"I know," I whisper.

We take my car instead, but halfway to the grocery store, a state trooper lights us up.

Routine stop. Broken taillight, we're certain, wasn't broken an hour earlier. The trooper is polite, apologetic, and meticulous.

Silence has learned to wear a uniform.

At home, I find my email flooded with meeting requests I didn't ask for and deadlines I didn't know existed. The task force agenda is revised—my speaking slot quietly moved to the end, then removed entirely.

"They're trying to exhaust you," Eric says.

"They're trying to make me choose," I reply.

That night, the dreams return. Not the water. Not the boats. Paper. Stacks of it, pressing down, sliding over mouths, smothering names until they blur into ink.

I wake with my heart racing and my throat sore, as if I've been screaming.

On the porch at dawn, I watch the park breathe in mist. For the first time since this began, fear sharpens into something closer to anger.

"How far will you go?" I ask the quiet.

The answer comes without heat.

As far as it has to.

Later that afternoon, Maribel calls, voice tight. "Someone contacted my aunt. Said our family should stop stirring things up if we care about our kids."

The line goes very still.

That's the escalation.

"They crossed a line," I say.

"Yes," she agrees. "So have we."

By evening, a flyer circulates online—anonymous, slickly designed—questioning my credibility, my motives, my mental health. *Grief can distort perception,* it reads.

Eric reads it twice, jaw set. "They're trying to turn you into the story."

"Then we take that away from them," I say.

I open my laptop and start drafting something I hadn't planned to yet.

A timeline. Names. Dates. Sources. Public. Verifiable. Shared. The hostile presence tightens, furious now, no longer pretending restraint. The lights flicker hard enough to pop.

Eric reaches for my hand. "If you do this, it won't stay theoretical."

"I know."

Outside, the cicadas cut off mid-song.

Silence has stopped negotiating.

And for the first time, it feels like it might actually be willing to hurt someone who isn't me.

Chapter Twenty-Seven

The Line That Wasn't There Before

I don't publish the timeline right away.

That hesitation costs us.

The first break-in doesn't look like a break-in at all. No shattered glass. No forced door. Just a back window unlocked when I know I latched it, the kitchen light left on, the faint smell of ozone lingering where it shouldn't.

Eric notices the smell first. He always does. "Electrical," he says quietly. "Something shorted."

"Or wanted us to think it did," I reply.

Nothing is taken. That's the point.

The message is everywhere else—drawers opened and closed again, notebooks stacked too neatly on the table, my binder returned to the shelf, but with one page missing. Only one. The page with the names written in the order they came to me.

My throat tightens. "They were here."

Eric checks the rooms, methodically and calmly, carrying the baseball bat we never thought we'd need. When he comes back, his face has gone pale in a way I don't like.

"They unplugged the router," he says. "And plugged it back in."

Silence wants us to know it can come and go.

I sit at the table and feel the house hold its breath. The park across the road is quiet tonight, darker than usual, the trees massed like a wall.

This is escalation, Josiah presses into me, steady and fierce. *It wants you to stop moving.*

"No," I whisper. "It wants us to be afraid."

Both.

Eric kneels in front of me, holding my hands, "We need to call the police."

"We can, and tell them what?" I say. "But listen to how it's been playing this. Nothing illegal. Nothing provable. Just pressure."

He nods slowly. "So we change the terrain."

That night, we don't sleep in the bedroom. We sit in the living room with lamps on and the curtains open, making ourselves visible. I uploaded the timeline to a secure drive, but haven't released it yet. Instead, I send it—quietly—to five people I trust. Journalists. Historians. A civil rights attorney whom Maribel connected me with.

"If anything happens to us," I write, "this goes public."

Eric squeezes my hand when he reads it. "You just took away their leverage."

"Some of it," I say.

The response is immediate.

Emails come back within minutes. *Received. Backed up. Understood.*

Silence shifts again, recalculating.

The next morning, the park gates are locked without notice. No signage. No explanation. A county cruiser idles near the entrance, engine running.

Maribel texts: **They're telling people it's for safety. No hazard listed.**

"Safety," Eric says bitterly. "From what?"

"From memory."

I go to school anyway.

Halfway through the second period, the fire alarm goes off again. This time it's inside the building. Students line up, annoyed, unconcerned. Outside, I spot the Miller near the front office, speaking in low tones to an administrator.

He doesn't look at me.

He doesn't have to.

During lunch, my phone buzzes with an alert I didn't set.

Unknown Device Logged In — Location: Nearby

My stomach drops.

"They're in our accounts now," Eric says when I show him. "Or trying to be."

The air in the classroom tightens, pressure blooming behind my eyes. I steady myself against the desk.

It is running out of clean options, Josiah tells me. *That makes it reckless.*

That afternoon, the call comes. This one doesn't bother with politeness.

"You need to stop," a man says, voice flat, untraceable. "You're putting people at risk."

"Who?" I ask.

A pause. Then, softly, "Your husband."

Eric's name is never spoken.

The line goes dead.

For a long moment, the world narrows to the sound of my own breathing. When I finally look up, the room feels tilted, like gravity has shifted.

I don't tell Eric right away. That's my mistake.

He finds out an hour later when his phone buzzes with a message containing nothing but a photo of his office building, taken from across the street and timestamped five minutes earlier. No threat. No caption. Proof of proximity.

Silence has drawn a new line.

Not around history.

Around us.

I feel Josiah surge, the calm restraint gone. *This is where it ends,* he says, *one way or another.*

I open the timeline again. This time, I don't hesitate. I schedule it. Public release. Midnight.

Silence wanted us isolated and afraid.

Instead, I am about to make us impossible for us to corner.

And somewhere between now and midnight, I know with a cold, steady certainty that it will try one last thing—something it won't be able to take back.

Chapter Twenty-Eight

Midnight Is a Trigger

At eleven forty-seven, the power flickers.

Not out. Just enough for the clocks on the stove and microwave to blink and reset, arguing briefly about what time it is before surrendering to zeroes.

Eric looks up from his phone. "They're trying to make us miss it."

"I set redundancies," I say. My voice is steady, but my pulse isn't. "Three servers. Two continents."

The house feels crowded with attention—every outlet humming, every wire awakens. Across the road, the park lies dark and quiet, but it's not empty. It's listening the way a held breath listens.

They'll push the network first, Josiah warns. *Then the people.*

At eleven fifty, my phone vibrates with a message from Maribel.

Maribel: The *County filed a request for a temporary injunction. Emergency filing. They're trying to stop publication.*

"Too late," Eric says, already refreshing feeds. "It's queued."

At eleven fifty-four, an unfamiliar car crawls past the house, slows, then continues. Headlights off. Not stealthy—*deliberate*. A reminder.

I stand and pull the curtains wide open. "We're not hiding."

The car doesn't come back.

At eleven fifty-eight, the internet drops.

Eric swears softly. "Cellular?"

"Hotspot," I say. "And—" My phone vibrates again. "—backup just went live."

The air tightens, then snaps. A sharp *pop* sounds from the breaker panel. The lights dim hard, then surge back to a brightness brighter than before. Somewhere in the house, glass chimes once, clean and loud.

Now, Josiah says. Not a warning—an alignment.

Midnight hits. For one second, nothing happens. Then everything does.

My phone explodes with notifications stacking faster than I can read.

Eric's screen fills with messages from people we don't know and some we do. The timeline is live. Names. Dates. Sources. The altered documents are side-by-side with the originals. Video from the springs. Audio from the forum. The map—routes traced in blue from Angola south, the Saltwater Railroad drawn plainly where silence tried to erase it.

"It's everywhere," Eric says, awe threading through fear. "They can't pull it back."

The house shudders.

Not metaphorically.

A deep vibration rolls up through the floor, rattling cabinets, setting the windows singing in their frames. Outside, the cicadas cut off in unison.

I stagger, catching the counter. "It's here."

It can't stop the truth, Josiah says, force gathering. *So, it will try to break the witnesses.*

The pressure slams inward—hard enough that my vision tunnels. A sound like a crowd shouting underwater fills my ears.

Images strobe, ledgers snap shut, stamps strike paper, hands tear maps in half. A door slams somewhere inside my head.

Eric grips my shoulders. "Gabby—stay with me."

"I'm here," I gasp. "I'm—"

The front door rattles. Not kicked. *Tested.* Once. Twice.

Eric moves without speaking, positioning himself between me and the door. His phone lights his face, pale and determined.

"Police?"

"They won't make it in time," I say, and realize with clarity that surprises me that I'm not afraid in the way I was before. "But we don't need them to."

I step forward and place my palm flat against the door.

Across the road, the park answers.

Not with sound—with *release*. A rush like water finding an old channel. The pressure shifts, drawn outward, away from the house, away from Eric. The ground hums low and deep, a note held by many voices.

I speak—not loudly, not for the door, but for the land. "Now."

The vibration swells, then breaks—like a knot loosening. The rattle stops. The hum fades to a steady, grounded quiet. Outside, the night exhales.

The door handle goes still.

Minutes pass. Then the car returns—this time with headlights on, moving too fast, disappearing down the road.

Eric's phone buzzes again. He reads, then looks up, disbelief cracking into relief. "The injunction was denied. Judge said there's 'overwhelming public interest.'"

I sink onto the couch, shaking now that the moment has passed. "It's done."

The lock is broken, Josiah says. His presence is different—no longer braced against resistance, no longer anchored to a single place. *What comes next will take time. But the door will not close again.*

Outside, the cicadas resume—tentative at first, then full, layered, alive. In the distance, sirens wail, late but coming.

Eric sits beside me and pulls me close. "They tried to scare us into quiet."

I lean into him, feeling the ordinary solidity of his heartbeat. "And failed."

On my phone, a message pushes to the top of the shared screen, shared thousands of times already:

We knew these stories. Thank you for saying the names.

Across the road, the park holds its shape in the dark—not a threat, not a secret. Just land, finally allowed to carry what it carries without punishment.

Midnight passed.

And the truth did what it has always done when it's finally let loose—it ran.

Chapter Twenty-Nine

What Comes After the Door Opens

Morning arrives without drama.

That surprises me most of all.

No sirens. No knocking. No official statement waiting like a reprimand on the porch. Just early light spilling through the kitchen window and the ordinary sound of Eric making coffee, the grinder too loud, the smell grounding.

I wake with the sense of having outrun something—and the quieter, heavier understanding that outrunning isn't the same as escaping.

The timeline has spread overnight.

Not just shared, but *adopted*. People have mirrored it, annotated it, and translated pieces into Spanish, Gullah Geechee, and Creole.

Someone built a public map layered with family stories, adding names I don't recognize and routes I never saw.

Silence can't pull back what it no longer owns.

Eric scrolls, shaking his head slowly. "They're trying to say it was inevitable."

"They always do," I say. "As if inevitability excuses delay."

By midmorning, the district releases a new statement, longer this time, full of words like *'reckoning' and 'healing'*. A commitment to review materials. A promise to consult with descendants. The historian's name is conspicuously absent.

"That's not accountability," Eric says.

"No," I agree. "But it's movement."

I go back to the park alone. Not to the clearing—yet—but to the edge of the springs where water moves slow and patient, unbothered by the attention it's suddenly receiving. Flowers line the path now, handwritten notes. Stones are arranged into names that will need to be relearned by those who placed them.

I kneel and touch the water. It's cold. Clean. Honest.

You did not open the door for me, Josiah says gently. *You opened it for them.*

"Does that mean you're done?" I ask.

A long pause, longer than before.

It means I am no longer bound to waiting.

The weight I've grown used to—like a hand resting between my shoulder blades—lightens further. Not gone, but no longer tethered to pain. He is present in the way memory is present when it stops hurting and starts teaching.

"I'm afraid of what happens next," I admit. "What they'll try."

They will try many things, he answers. *But they will not be able to make it small again.*

At home, Eric fields a call from a legal aid group offering protection, representation, and resources we didn't know existed until we needed them. Another from a museum director asking about an exhibit—*with names,* she emphasizes.

Eric covers the phone and looks at me. "This is turning into a life."

"I know."

He smiles, tired and proud. "Good."

That afternoon, Maribel sends a photo.

A marker—temporary, wooden, hastily carved—stands near the springs.

ANGOLA

A MAROON SETTLEMENT

DESTROYED, NOT LOST

I sit with that for a long time.

Not lost.

Destroyed.

Words matter.

As evening falls, the park fills again—quietly, respectfully. No chanting. No speeches. Just people walking, reading, listening. I stand at the edge and let myself be one of them.

The cicadas sing without interruption.

For the first time since we moved here, the land feels like land—not a wound demanding attention, not a secret demanding protection.

Eric slips his hand into mine. "You ready for the next fight?"

I think of classrooms. Of students asking better questions. Of records that will resist correction because resistance is what they do.

"Yes," I say. "But not tonight."

We walk home together, the road no longer a boundary, just a crossing.

Behind us, the springs keep moving.

Ahead of us, the work waits, hard, necessary, unfinished.

And somewhere between the two, Josiah finally steps back— not erased, not forgotten, but free enough to let others carry the way forward.

The door is open. Now comes the living.

Chapter Thirty

What Refuses to Settle

The thing about the aftermath is that it doesn't look like an ending.

It looks like meetings.

It looks like emails that begin with *following up' and 'circling back'*. It seems like promises made carefully, with enough room left inside them to wriggle away later if no one is watching. Which means someone has to watch.

The first official walk-through of the park happens on a humid Thursday morning. County representatives. A university archaeologist. Two people introduced as "community liaisons" who keep glancing at Maribel before speaking. Clipboards everywhere. So many clipboards.

I'm there as an observer, which is its own kind of fiction.

"You won't interfere," one of the county officials says, smiling tightly.

"I won't interrupt," I reply. "Interference depends on intent."

Eric stands by my side and bites back a laugh.

The limestone shelf is submerged again, but the water is lower than it used to be. The archaeologist kneels at the edge, murmuring to herself, fingers hovering just above the surface.

"There's a disturbance here," she says finally. "Human-made. Repeated use."

"Departure," Maribel says.

The official opens his mouth—then closes it again. Someone writes something down.

Good.

That afternoon, Harold Miller's resignation becomes public. No explanation. Just a short notice thanking the historian for his years of service.

Silence doesn't apologize. It sheds skin.

Eric reads the announcement twice. "They're hoping that's enough."

"It isn't," I say. "But it's a start."

At school, my classroom feels different.

Students sit forward now. They don't just ask what happened; they ask how it was hidden. They bring stories from home—half-remembered warnings, family sayings that suddenly make sense.

"Why didn't they teach this?" one student asks.

"Because history isn't just about the past," I answer. "It's about power."

After class, a young black girl waits until the room empties.

"My great-grandmother said not to trust official maps," she tells me softly. "She said the real ones were in people."

I swallow. "She was right."

That night, I dream—but gently.

Not of fire or pressure or voices pushing through my ribs. I dream of water moving under moonlight, steady and unafraid. Canoes pass without urgency. No one is chasing them.

When I wake, Josiah is there—but only just.

This is the part where I learn how to leave without leaving, he says.

"You don't have to go," I tell him, surprised by the catch in my voice.

I know, a pause, warm with gratitude. *But staying isn't the same as being trapped anymore.*

The hostile presence doesn't surge. It doesn't strike. It lingers instead. Reduced now to resistance in meeting minutes, to footnotes that hedge, to funding requests that take too long.

Manageable.

Mortal.

Eric and I sit on the porch after sunset, watching fireflies blink in uneven patterns.

"Do you think they'll really change the records?" he asks.

"Yes," I say. "Slowly. In pieces. And some of it they'll never admit outright."

"That bother you?"

I shake my head. "Truth doesn't need permission to exist. It just needs witnesses."

Across the road, the park breathes evenly. No silence falling. No warning hum. Just insects and wind and the low sound of water doing what it's always done.

This isn't peace. It's vigilance without fear.

And that, I'm learning, might be the truest kind of resolution history ever allows.

Chapter Thirty-One

What Is Finally Named

The marker changes on a Tuesday.

Not announced. Not ceremonious. Just quietly replaced sometime between dusk and dawn, as if the land itself got tired of waiting.

I notice it on my way to work, the way you see a familiar face has aged overnight. The temporary wooden sign is gone. In its place stands something sturdier—metal, clean-lined, unmistakably official.

ANGOLA

A maroon settlement established by self-emancipated people. Destroyed during U.S. military campaigns in 1821.
This site marks both loss and resistance.

I pull over without thinking.

Other cars are already there. A woman photographs the sign with shaking hands. A man stands with his hat pressed to his chest, lips moving in silent prayer. No one speaks. No one needs to.

Eric texts me from his office.

Eric: *They updated the state database. It's live.*

I close my eyes and breathe.

This is how it happens—not with absolution, not with apology, but with permanence. Words anchored where erasure once stood.

At school, the bell rings and rings again before anyone settles. Students buzz with it, phones passed hand to hand, screenshots pulled up like proof of existence.

"They admitted it," one boy says, half awed.

"They didn't admit enough," another counters.

Both are right.

During my planning period, I received an email from the museum director. The subject line reads simply: *Exhibit Confirmation.*

Names will be included. Routes mapped. Descendant voices recorded in their own words.

With attribution, the email emphasizes.

Good.

That afternoon, I walked to the park again—not as a witness this time, but as a participant in something that has outgrown me. The water is high today, the limestone shelf hidden once more, but I know it's there. Everyone does now.

Josiah waits near the edge of my awareness, lighter than ever.

They know where we stood, he says. *That is enough.*

"Are you ready?" I ask.

A smile moves through me that isn't mine alone.

I have been ready since the boats left, he answers. *I just needed someone to remember why.*

The weight lifts—not suddenly, not dramatically—but completely like a hand unclenching after holding too tight for too long. The air feels wider. The park sounds fuller.

Josiah doesn't vanish. He changes.

He settles into the land the way a story settles once it's been told properly, not haunting, not demanding, simply present. Available to anyone who listens without fear.

Eric finds me there as the sun dips low, the sky turning the color of old paper.

"They asked if you'd consult long-term," he says. "Curriculum, public history."

I think of my classroom. Of students leaning forward. Of names spoken aloud without trembling.

"Yes," I say. "But on my terms."

He smiles. "I figured."

We stand together at the edge of the springs, watching water move over memory without drowning it.

The truth didn't free everyone.

It never does.

But it freed the story from silence.

And that, I've learned, is how history finally breathes—not erased, not avenged, but named.

At last.

Chapter Thirty-Two

What We Carry Forward

The semester ends without ceremony.

No grand announcement. No final headline. Just grades submitted, classrooms stripped back to cinderblock and dust, the quiet ritual of closing a door on a year that changed more than it taught.

On the last day, my students leave behind things they didn't bring in with them—questions still forming, stories they plan to ask for at home, the understanding that history isn't finished when the bell rings.

One boy pauses at the doorway. "Are we going to keep learning this next year?"

"Yes," I say. "You are."

He grins like it's a promise and not a responsibility.

At the park, the path to the springs is busier now, but softer. People move with intention. They read the marker. They leave stones and notes and sometimes nothing at all, which feels just as respectful.

A small placard announces upcoming archaeological work and community days—*descendant-led*, it specifies.

Words matter. They always have.

Eric and I walk the trail in the evenings when the heat loosens its grip. We talk about ordinary things again—grocery lists, vacation days, the neighbor's loud dog—without pretending the extraordinary hasn't threaded itself through us.

"You know," he says one night, "I used to think justice was something you won. Like a case. A verdict."

"And now?"

"And now it feels more like maintenance," he says. "You don't fix it once. You keep showing up."

I nod. "That's history too."

The museum exhibit opens quietly. Then loudly. Descendants arrive from places the Saltwater Railroad once pointed toward—the Keys, Bahamas, Cuba. They recognize names, routes, and each other. They argue about details and agree about meaning. They laugh. They cry. They take photos beside maps that no longer pretend the water was empty.

I attend as a consultant, not a centerpiece. That feels right. Josiah doesn't come to me as often now.

When he does, it's without urgency, without the old pull of waiting. He's present the way a remembered voice is present—clear when called, gentle when not.

One evening, as the sky bruises into dusk, I stop at the edge of the springs and say what I've been holding back.

"Thank you."

The land answers with nothing dramatic. Just water moving the way it always has.

You listened, Josiah says. *That was enough.*

"And now?"

A pause—warm, satisfied.

Now you carry it. Not alone.

The cicadas rise and fall. Fireflies blink in the understory like punctuation marks.

At home, I box up my notes—not to hide them, not to lock them away, but to make room. New syllabi. New questions. The work ahead isn't lighter, but it's clearer.

Silence still exists. It always will. It lives in budgets and delays, and the temptation to move on too quickly.

But it no longer owns this story.

On the porch, Eric slips an arm around me as the night settles.

"What happens if they try again?" he asks.

I watch the road, the park beyond it, the land that no longer flinches when named.

"Then we remember," I say. "Out loud."

Across the springs, water carries moonlight south, steady and unafraid.

The Saltwater Railroad isn't a secret anymore. It's a lesson. And like all lessons that matter, it doesn't end—it moves, carried forward by those willing to listen, to speak, and to stay.

Chapter Thirty-Three

What Doesn't Let Go Easily

The first warning comes dressed as opportunity.
It arrives in a polished envelope with a Tallahassee return address, the paper heavier than it needs to be. An invitation—*no, a request*—for me to serve on a statewide advisory panel on "Contested Regional Narratives." The language is flattering. The subtext is not.

Eric reads it twice. "This is a leash."

"Yes," I say. "A longer one."

I don't respond right away. Silence has learned that patience can look like cooperation, and I refuse to teach that lesson again.

Two days later, the park fence goes up.
Not around the springs—around a section of land just east of them, an area no one has paid attention to because nothing official ever acknowledged what was there. Survey flags appear overnight, pink and orange wounds against the green.

Maribel calls before I see it myself. "They're saying it's for soil testing."

My stomach tightens. "Testing for what?"

"That's the problem," she says. "No one will say."

When I arrive, a uniformed contractor blocks the path.

"Restricted access."

"Under whose authority?" I ask.

He shrugs. "State."

That word again. Big enough to hide inside.

The land reacts.

Not violently. Not openly. The cicadas stutter. Birds lift and don't settle again. The air thickens, heavy with a pressure I haven't felt since before the reckoning.

Josiah presses close for the first time in weeks—sharper, more urgent.

They are trying to take the ground itself, he says. *If they own it, they will decide what it remembers.*

A chill runs through me. "Eminent domain?"

Something like it, he answers. *Paper can still kill what guns cannot.*

That night, the museum director emails me, frantic. A grant review has been "paused." Funding contingent on "reassessment of interpretive framing."

They're no longer denying the history. They're containing it.

Eric paces the living room. "They waited just long enough for people to relax."

"Yes," I say. "That's how you know it matters."

The second warning is quieter—and closer.

Someone files a formal complaint with the district alleging that my curriculum is "politically coercive." The language is precise and legal, but preloaded with citations that don't quite apply. An investigator is assigned. Interviews scheduled.

"They're building a record," Eric says.

"They're trying to make me radioactive," I reply.

Outside, headlights slow in front of the house again. Not the same car as before. A different one. Daylight this time.

I don't flinch. Instead, I do the thing silence hates most.

I call a meeting.

Not official. Not permitted. At the park pavilion—still technically open, still legally public. Descendants. Journalists. A land-use attorney recommended by the civil rights group. A hydrologist who knows precisely what happens when water levels are manipulated for "testing."

People come faster than I expect.

So does the state.

A cease-and-desist order arrives mid-meeting, printed and hand-delivered. No police. Just paper. Just pressure.

I read it aloud.

Then I hand it to the attorney, who smiles without humor. "They're late."

The cameras roll. Phones lift. Someone starts recording the survey flags behind the fence, the timing, the contradiction.

Josiah steadies—not anchored to me now, but to the gathering itself.

This is why I stayed, he says. *Because silence always tries again.*

A county worker I've never met steps forward. "Those surveys weren't approved," she says, voice shaking but firm. "They were rushed."

A second worker nods. "They skipped protocol."

Cracks spread.

Eric leans close. "You okay?"

I nod, though my pulse is racing. "They're escalating."

"So are we."

As dusk falls, the meeting disperses—not scattered, not afraid, but organized. Tasks assigned. Records requested. Oversight demanded.

The fence still stands.

For now.

But the land hums beneath it, restless and awake, and I understand the final truth about silence:

It never gives up.

It just hopes you will.

I look across the springs, at the water carrying moonlight south the way it always has, and feel Josiah's presence not as a warning, but a resolve.

"Then we don't," I say quietly.

And somewhere, deep inside the machinery of power that thought this story was finished, something shifts—uneasy now, aware that the ground beneath it has learned how to resist.

Chapter Thirty-Four

What It Costs to Hold the Line

The injunction comes at sunrise.

Not delivered, not announced. It appears in the system the way fog appears on water—quiet, total, pretending it has always been there. By the time I open my email, it's already been forwarded to half a dozen inboxes with *URGENT* stamped across the top like a bruise.

Temporary Restraining Order. All activity, assembly, and dissemination related to the Angola site is to cease pending review.

Eric reads it aloud once, then again, slower. "Cease assembly," he says. "They're trying to make gathering itself illegal."

"They're trying to turn presence into trespass," I answer.

Outside, the fence still stands. The orange mesh glows obscene in the morning light, too bright for a place that has learned how to hold shadow.

A county truck idles where it shouldn't. Men in vests pretend not to watch the house.

Josiah presses close—not heavy, not urgent, but focused, like a hand steadying a blade.

This is the narrowing, he says, *when they decide whether the story survives because you endure—or because you're erased.*

My phone buzzes. Then buzzes again. Maribel. The attorney. Two reporters. A number I don't recognize.

I don't answer any of them yet.

Instead, I walk across the road.

Eric catches my arm. "The order—"

"Doesn't apply to walking," I say. "Not yet."

The air thickens as I cross the pavement. The park feels different this morning—alert, not braced. The cicadas start and stop, unsure. The fence hums faintly, metal talking to the ground in a language it was never meant to learn.

I stop ten feet from the mesh.

On the other side, survey flags mark neat grids, pink and orange wounds stitched into the earth. Someone has chalked numbers on limestone that has never belonged to numbers.

"This isn't safety," I say aloud. "This is erasure with a deadline."

A man clears his throat behind me. A worker I recognize—one who spoke up at the pavilion—stands with his hat in his hands.

"They rushed the paperwork," he says quietly. "Skipped environmental review. Skipped tribal consultation. Skipped descendants."

"On purpose," I say.

He nods. "They think speed will outrun opposition."

I think of canoes pushing off under moonlight. Of running not to escape, but to arrive somewhere else.

"No," I say. "They think speed will exhaust us."

By noon, the consequences arrive like weather.

The museum emails to say the exhibit opening is postponed "pending legal clarity."

The school district has scheduled an "investigatory interview" for Friday, with the agenda undisclosed.

Eric's reopened compliance file expands—new requests, older dates, a fishing net cast backward in time.

"They're bleeding us from every angle," Eric says, pacing. "Money. Reputation. Time."

"They're testing endurance," I reply. "Not truth."

At one-thirty, the first patrol car parks across from the house. Not lights. Not confrontation. Just presence.

I sit at the table and feel my hands start to shake.

Josiah steadies me. *Breathe. This is where they expect fear to do the work for them.*

"Okay," I whisper. "Then we work smarter." I open my laptop and do the thing I've been avoiding.

I make it bigger. Not louder—broader.

By three o'clock, the timeline is mirrored on four international servers. A public call goes out—not for protest, not for assembly, but for *testimony*. Written. Recorded. Sworn. Descendants invited to submit statements under penalty of perjury, preserved in an independent archive.

"They can shut down a gathering," Eric says slowly. "They can't shut down affidavits."

"And if they try," I add, "they admit exactly what this is."

The response is slower than before—but deeper.

Stories arrive measured and careful, names paired with dates. Routes sketched from memory and corroborated by ship logs and wreckers' manifests. One submission includes a brittle photograph of a woman standing beside a canoe, back straight, eyes defiant.

Ruth, Josiah breathes, and the name carries not grief now, but recognition.

At dusk, the suits return.

This time, they don't smile.

"The order stands," the woman says. "You're risking contempt."

I step onto the porch so the cameras can see me clearly. "Then put it in writing that the state is preventing descendants from submitting sworn testimony about their own history."

She hesitates—just a fraction.

Cameras love fractions.

Eric stands beside me. "We've complied with the order," he says evenly. "No assembly. No protest. Just speech."

"Speech can be restrained," the man with the tablet says.

"Not like this," the attorney says from behind the camera. "Not without a hearing."

The woman's jaw tightens. "You're making this adversarial."

I nod. "You made it adversarial when you fenced memory."

Night comes down fast.

The patrol car's engine keeps running.

Inside, exhaustion finally claws its way through my resolve. I sink onto the couch, head in my hands.

"What if they win by attrition?" I ask, the fear slipping out before I can stop it. "What if we can't keep this pace?"

Eric sits beside me, solid, familiar. "Then we slow it down," he says. "We don't stop."

Josiah's presence warms—not to console, but to remind.

This is the cost of holding the line, he says. *Not glory. Not relief. Time.*

Later, alone at the window, I watch the fence catch moonlight and think we're not close to finished.

That's the point.

Silence never gives up in a single night. It waits for fatigue, for doubt, for the moment when the living decide the dead have had enough attention.

I straighten.

"Not yet," I say to the dark. "Not ever."

Across the road, beneath mesh and markers and men who think they own what can be measured, the ground hums back—steady, patient, alive.

We will outlast them.

We always have.

Chapter Thirty-Five

When the Descendants Arrive

They come anyway.

Not in buses. Not in a march. They arrive the way people do when they're answering something older than instruction—one car at a time, plates from counties and states that trace the Saltwater Railroad without ever naming it. Florida Keys. Georgia. South Carolina. Alabama. A rental with Bahamian plates still dusted with salt.

By midmorning, the shoulder along the road is full.

No one crosses the fence. That detail matters. They stand just outside it, close enough to see the survey flags, far enough to deny the state its easiest excuse. Children sit on tailgates. Elders lean on canes and hoods and the steady arms of younger relatives. Some people hold folders. Others hold nothing but folded paper worn thin at the creases.

The air thickens—not with anger, not yet—but with gravity.

Eric counts quietly beside me. "Thirty. No—forty."

"More," I say. "They're still coming."

Josiah presses close, and for the first time since the injunction, his presence carries something like awe.

They followed the way back, he says, *even when it was never written down.*

Maribel arrives last, parking crooked because there's nowhere else to fit. She steps out and looks at the gathering, eyes shining.

"They tried to stop the meeting," she says. "So, people turned it into a return."

The patrol car across the road shifts position. Another joins it. No lights. No sirens. Just weight.

I feel it then—the tension that hums beneath skin, the kind that comes before a storm breaks or a crowd decides which way it will move. Silence is here too, taut and alert, recalculating faster than before.

This is not what it planned for.

A woman steps forward, staying firmly on the public side of the fence. She holds up a laminated photograph—black-and-white, edges soft with age.

"My name is Althea Moss," she says, voice steady despite the way her hands tremble. "My great-grandmother ran from Angola. She never said the word. She just said *we left by water*."
She turns the photo so others can see. A woman stands beside a canoe, back straight, chin lifted, daring the world to contradict her presence.

"I'm submitting testimony," Althea continues. "Here. Today." She hands the folder to the attorney, who nods and records the time.

That breaks something open.

A man follows, then another. Names spoken. Dates offered with caveats and care. Routes described with hands tracing air where maps once refused to show anything but blank space.

"I don't know his birth year," someone says. "But I know when he stopped being afraid."

A child asks quietly, "Is this where they left?"

"Yes," I answer before anyone can stop me. "This is one of the places."

The woman from the car with Bahamian plates waits until the crowd settles before stepping forward and speaking.

Not because she's nervous—but because she knows the value of pause.

"My Name is Sylvia Johnson. My great-grandmother used to say," The woman begins, her voice rounded by a Bahamian lilt that bends the words gently, "that the water don't forget who trust it."

Heads lift. People lean in.

She stands straight, hands folded at her waist, eyes bright and steady. Sunlight catches the silver threads in her hair. She is not reading. She doesn't need notes.

"She never called it Angola," she continues. "She called it *the place we had to leave fast*. But she always said we left *together*."

A murmur moves through the listeners.

"She said they pushed the boats out at night. No lights. No talking. Just hands and breath and the sound of water moving under them like it already knew the way."

The woman smiles softly at something only she can see.

"My great-grandmother was a girl then. She said the boat smelled like fear and wood and salt. She said the men took turns watching the stars—one low, one steady—because the stars don't lie, even when maps do."

She pauses, letting that land.

"They didn't go north because north had people waiting for them," she says plainly. "Men with dogs. Men with papers. Men who believed they owned what they could catch."

Several heads nod. It was a familiar story.

"They went south because the water was wide. Because the British wreckers didn't ask too many questions. Because once you crossed far enough, the rules changed."

Her voice tightens just slightly.

"She said the sea was rough. She said some people prayed, some sang, and some did both at the same time. She said one woman held a baby the whole way and never sat down, even when her arms shook."

The crowd is very still now.

"When they reached the Bahamas, she said the land felt sharp under her feet—coral instead of mud—but nobody chased them.

Nobody counted them. Nobody asked for papers."

The woman lifts her chin.

"They were hungry. They were scared. But they were *there*."

She exhales, slow and deliberate.

"She grew up free. Not easy. Free ain't easy. But free enough to choose. Free enough to tell the story."

The woman looks around now, meeting eyes.

"She told it to my grandmother. My grandmother told it to my mother. My mother told it to me, but always in a soft voice. Always like a warning wrapped inside a lullaby."

Her voice steadies, gains strength.

"They told us not to forget the water. They told us to remember that sometimes freedom don't look like land—it look like risk."

She steps back from the invisible line where a microphone might be.

"I came here because I heard the names being spoken," she says. "And because my great-grandmother said, if anybody ever say the place wasn't real—tell them we are."

Silence holds for a long moment.

Then someone whispers, "Thank you."

The woman nods once.

Across the road, beyond trees and time and the narrowness of maps, the springs move south—toward salt, toward islands, toward a shore where a frightened girl once stepped onto coral and learned what it meant to arrive.

The Saltwater Railroad did not end at the water's edge.

It crossed.

And it still crosses now every time the story is told out loud.

The fence hums faintly, metal complaining against earth. Across it, the survey flags flutter as if they're trying to pull free.

State officials arrive at noon.

Three vehicles. Four people. All wearing expressions designed to calm. One of them—a man with a badge I recognize from earlier meetings—takes in the crowd and stiffens.

"This gathering violates the spirit of the injunction," he says carefully.

"No," the attorney replies. "It honors the letter of it. No assembly. No protest. Individual testimony submitted lawfully."

The man's gaze flicks to me. "You organized this."

"I didn't," I say. "History did."

A murmur ripples—not applause, not defiance. Recognition.

Josiah steadies, no longer anchored me alone. His presence threads through the people standing here, through the names being spoken aloud without fear of punishment.

This is what silence cannot stop, he says. *Return.*

The officials retreat to their vehicles to make calls. The patrol cars idle harder, engines loud enough to remind everyone of consequence.

The tension spikes when a young man steps too close to the fence, his foot brushing the mesh.

A trooper moves instantly. "Sir—"

Eric steps forward without thinking. "He didn't cross."

The trooper hesitates.

Cameras catch it. The pause. The calculation.

The young man steps back, jaw clenched. "I just wanted to see where my people stood."

"You are seeing it," Maribel says softly. "From here."

The heat builds. Sweat slicks spines. Water bottles pass hand to hand. Still, no one leaves.

This is the part that silence doesn't understand.

People will endure discomfort when they are no longer alone in it.

By late afternoon, the affidavit count passes one hundred.

By dusk, two hundred.

Some stories overlap. Some contradict. That's how truth looks when it's finally allowed to be complex.

Eric leans close. "They're not going to be able to pretend this is isolated."

"That's why they're scared," I whisper back.

As the sun drops, someone begins to hum. Low at first. Wordless. A sound older than hymns, older than policy. Others join, hesitant at first, then steadier. The song doesn't cross the fence—but it fills the space above it, settles into the trees, rides the evening air toward the water.

The patrol cars don't move.

The officials don't return.

Silence holds—tight, strained, thinning.

I feel Josiah loosen again, not disappearing, not leaving, but stepping back the way someone does when a watch has ended.

You held the line, he tells me. *Now they will have to answer it.*

Night falls.

The descendants don't disperse all at once. They leave in clusters, touching the ground before they go, pressing palms to earth that finally knows their names.

The fence still stands.

But it looks smaller now.

And beneath it, beneath the paperwork and pressure and men who thought time was on their side, the ground hums—patient, collective, unafraid.

This is no longer a story being told.

It is a presence that has returned.

And silence is running out of places to hide.

Chapter Thirty-Six

What Silence Tries One Last Time

I have watched erasure learn every language it needs to know.

I watched it speak in gunfire and firelight, when it believed fear alone would be enough. I watched it grow patient when fear proved unreliable, watched it learn ink and paper and signatures that could travel farther than soldiers ever did. I watched it understand, slowly, that killing bodies is inefficient when you can starve memory instead.

This is its last lesson.

Silence does not rage when it is about to lose. It narrows. It sharpens itself to a single point and drives that point where it believes the living will finally bend.

Tonight, that point is fear.

The men return after midnight. Not the ones in uniform. Not the ones who smile for cameras. These wear neither badge nor insignia. They move like people accustomed to believing the land will not challenge them. Their boots are quiet. Their flashlights were hooded. Their confidence was practiced.

They do not step beyond the fence.

That matters.

They have learned where the line is now, and they do not cross it unless they must.

Instead, they work the perimeter.

They take down the temporary marker first—the wooden one placed by hands that trembled but did not stop. It splinters easily. They leave the pieces where they fall, a deliberate mess meant to look careless. Accidental. As if the land itself rejected the memory.

One of them laughs. The sound is thin.

I gather myself where limestone meets water, where my blood once ran warm and then ran out. I am not bound the way I was, not anchored by waiting. I am held now by witness. That is new.

They move next to the survey flags, yanking several free and tossing them into the springs. Pink and orange disappear beneath the surface, color leaching into dark water like a bruise spreading. The man with the light pauses, watching them sink. "See?" he murmurs to the others. "Gone."

That is the lie they have always told themselves.

Gone.

I reach for the water.

Not to rise. Not to frighten. Fear is a blunt tool, and silence has already dulled it through overuse. Instead, I press memory outward—quietly, deliberately—into the space they think belongs only to them.

The temperature drops. Just enough.

The man with the light shivers. He rubs his arms. "You feel that?"

"Humidity," another answers. "Move."

They unroll a banner next.

Canvas. Official seal. The kind meant for press conferences and ribbon cuttings.

SITE CLOSED — SAFETY REVIEW IN PROGRESS

They hang it crooked, the way people do when they want disrespect to pass as efficiency. One of them takes a photograph. Documentation. Proof of compliance.

Silence loves proof.

I let them finish.

That is important too.

Then I speak—not with sound, not with image, but with alignment.

The ground answers. Not violently. Not suddenly. The limestone shelf shifts a fraction of an inch, enough to unsettle footing without causing harm, a reminder, not a threat. The water ripples outward in concentric rings with no visible source.

The man with the light swears softly.

"Wind," someone says, too quickly.

The banner snaps once in the air, and it hasn't moved.

They leave then, faster than they arrived, careful again, professionalism restored. No one runs. Silence never runs. By morning, the message is meant to be clear.

You can gather.

You can speak.

But we can still reach the place itself.

They believe land can be intimidated.

They always have.

What they do not understand—what they never learned, because they never listened—is that land remembers differently than people do. It does not flinch. It waits. It absorbs and returns pressure slowly, inexorably.

By dawn, the descendants arrive again.

They notice everything.

The broken marker.

The missing flags.

The banner hung crooked like a threat that didn't land cleanly.

No one shouts.

That is what silence expects. Outrage. Reaction. Something it can point to and call disorder.

Instead, a woman kneels where the marker stood and places her palm flat against the dirt.

"They were here," she says quietly.

"Yes," another answers. "But so were we."

They do not replace the marker.

They do something more dangerous.

They begin to write.

Names on paper weighted with stones. Names pressed into the ground with sticks and fingertips. Names spoken aloud without amplification, without permission.

The banner flaps uselessly behind them.

This is when silence panics.

Not loudly. Internally. It floods systems with urgency. Calls are made. Emails sent. Language escalates from *review* to *violation*.

The machinery turns faster than it should, and that speed exposes it.

A state vehicle arrives, then another. Officials step out with clipped voices and legal phrases ready.

"This area is closed," one says.

A man holding his grandmother's name written carefully in pencil looks up. "We're not inside."

The official hesitates.

I feel the moment tilt.

This is the edge silence cannot step past without revealing itself completely. Force would fracture the mask. Retreat would concede ground. It chooses intimidation.

A woman in a suit steps forward. "If you continue," she says evenly, "there will be consequences."

"For who?" someone asks.

The woman opens her mouth. No name comes out.

That is the failure. That is the crack.

I move then—not forward, not outward, but through, not through air or earth, but through memory that no longer belongs to me alone. I let my name surface in many mouths at once. Not shouted, not demanded.

Recognized.

Josiah.

The sound moves across the gathering like breath, like a shared exhale. The officials freeze—not because they hear me, but because they feel the shift they cannot explain.

Silence recoils.

This is the last thing it knows how to do.

It threatens consequences without specificity. It promises delay. It invokes authority that no longer commands the same obedience. Then it withdraws. Not defeated, but exposed.

I feel the attempt loosen and fall away like a hand that finally realizes it is empty.

This was the final intimidation.

Not the strongest.

The most desperate.

I stand now where I fell then, not to guard a way out, but to watch a way forward that no longer needs me to hold it alone.

The living have learned something important.

Erasure only works when it is quiet.

And quiet is no longer available to them.

When the descendants leave that evening, they do not take the names with them. They leave them where the land can keep them.

I feel myself lighten—not vanish, not end, but settle into something that does not ache.

Silence will try again someday. It always does.

But it will not find this place unguarded.

Not by me.

Not by them.

Not ever again.

Chapter Thirty-Seven

1821: The Year the Names Were Taken

They chose the date deliberately.

1821.

Not because it's neat. Not because it's commemorated. But because it is the year Angola was not just attacked—but **ended**.

The year the raid scattered what remained. The year people vanished so completely that the record pretended they had never gathered there at all.

The year silence thought it had won.

The stage is temporary—wooden risers set just outside the fence, microphones powered by generators that hum like insects trapped in metal. The injunction still exists on paper, so everything is placed with care: public road, public space, public witness.

No banners.

No slogans.

Just a lectern and a stack of pages thick enough to feel like a body when I lift them.

Eric stands in the front row, one hand folded around the program, the other loose at his side but ready. Maribel stands

beside him. County workers, I recognize. Descendants, I don't—
yet, journalists who understand now that this isn't performance.

The crowd stretches farther than I expect, lining the shoulder of
the road, quiet in a way that hums under the skin.

I step to the microphone. For a moment, time presses close—
not violently, not urgently, but insistently. Like the tide testing the
shore.

1821.

The year the Creek raiders came south.

The year homes burned.

The year, over three hundred people were taken, and hundreds
more scattered by water, fear, and necessity.
The year Angola ceased to exist as a place anyone was supposed to
remember.

I clear my throat.

"We are here to read names," I say. "Not as an accusation. Not
as an apology. As a fact."

The microphone crackles once, then steadies.

"These names appear in fragments—military reports, shipping
logs, letters, oral histories, church margins, family Bibles. Some
are incomplete. Some contradict each other. That does not make
them less real."

I look down at the first page.

My hands shake. I let them.

"Eli Freeman."

The sound moves through the crowd like a breath finally
released.

"Ruth Freeman."

Someone sobs—not loud enough to interrupt, loud enough to be
heard.

"Samuel Boatwright."

I pause between each name. Not for emphasis. For **space**. For the dignity of not rushing what was once erased in haste.

Behind me, a screen displays nothing but text. No dates yet. No explanations. Just names appearing as they're spoken, black letters against white.

A woman in the third row whispers, "That's my family."

Another voice answers, "Mine too."

As the list grows, the air changes. Not in a way I would have recognized months ago. This isn't fear. This is **weight redistributing**—like a structure settling into place after being forced to carry too much alone.

Halfway through, I stop.

"This next group comes from testimony describing what happened *after* the raid," I say. "After Angola was destroyed. After families fled south by water."

I don't say *Saltwater Railroad*. Everyone here already knows the way.

"Some of these people were never recorded again. Others reappear decades later in places that should not connect—unless you know the route."

I read more slowly now.

Names followed by pauses long enough to feel like absences.

Names without surnames.

Names marked *possibly, believed, remembered as*.

This is where 1821 lives—not only in violence, but in what followed it, in the deliberate confusion. The scattering meant to ensure no one could ever stand in one place and answer roll call again.

Eric meets my eyes. He nods once.

I keep going.

By the time I reach the final pages, the sun has dropped low enough to stretch shadows across the road. The fence behind us glows dull orange, diminished now by how many eyes refuse to look away from the lectern.

I reach the last name. I don't expect it to stop me. It does anyway.

"Josiah."

I don't plan the pause.

The crowd doesn't move. Doesn't speak. Doesn't need to.

For the first time since this began, I feel him not as presence, not as pressure—but as **release**. Not gratitude. Something quieter. Completion without disappearance.

"We read these names today," I say, my voice steady now, "because in 1821 they were meant to be lost. And because silence only survives when no one answers it."

I step back.

There is no applause.

Instead, the crowd answers the way it has learned to.

"Here."

"Present."

"Remembered."

The words move outward, not rehearsed, not organized—alive.

Behind us, the land holds steady. No hum. No warning. Just ground that has finally been allowed to keep what it always carried.

Later, when the equipment is packed away, and the officials retreat and the road empties, Eric and I sit on the porch and watch night settle.

"You changed something today," he says quietly.

"No," I answer. "We corrected it."

Across the road, beyond the fence that no longer feels permanent, the springs move south, carrying moonlight the way they always have.

1821 was meant to end the story.

It didn't.

Because names—once spoken aloud—do not return to silence.

Not ever.

Chapter Thirty-Eight

What Cannot Be Put Back

The fence comes down three days later.

Not ceremonially. Not with apology. A county crew arrives just after sunrise, orange vests bright against the trees, movements brisk and deliberately ordinary. Bolts clatter into buckets. Mesh sags, then folds. By the time most people wake up, the line that tried to redefine the land is gone.

Someone films it anyway. By noon, the footage is everywhere.

"They're calling it a procedural correction," Eric says, reading from his phone. Improper permitting. Incomplete review."

I watch the last post lever free of the ground. The earth resists for a moment—then releases it with a soft, final sound. "They're calling it whatever lets them keep their jobs."

"That enough for you?" Eric said.

"No," I say. "But it's movement."

Movement brings attention. Attention brings consequence. By midafternoon, a formal notice arrives: a public hearing scheduled in two weeks to determine permanent protections for the site. Descendant testimony invited. Archaeological review mandated. Curriculum revisions "under consideration."

Silence is retreating into process.

That's dangerous territory for it—process leaves paper trails.

At school, the halls feel different again. Not charged this time—attentive. A colleague stops me between classes, eyes bright, voice low. "I didn't know how to talk about it before," she says. "But my students won't stop asking."

"Good," I answer. "Neither should you."

The investigator assigned to my case emails that evening. The subject line reads *Status Update*. The body is brief: *No further action recommended at this time.*

At this time, it is doing a lot of work.

Eric exhales when I show him. "They're backing off."

"They're regrouping," I say. "Same thing. Different phase."

We walk to the springs at dusk. The path is open again, trampled soft by the passage of people who came and stayed and left marks you can't photograph. Someone has placed stones along the water's edge, each etched with a name. Not permanent. Intentionally so.

"Do you want to keep this?" Eric asks.

I think of the affidavits. The recordings. The way the names traveled once they were spoken aloud. "It doesn't belong to us anymore," I say. "That's how it survives."

Josiah comes to me one last time—not as a weight, not as a warning, but as a witness stepping back.

This is the part I never saw, he tells me. *The living choosing care over fear.*

"Will you stay?" I ask, though I already know the answer.

I'll be where memory rests when it's treated gently, he says. *Not where it's used as a weapon.*

The air warms where he had been. The water keeps moving.

At home, the phone rings—an unfamiliar number. A state office. A careful voice offering a seat on a committee that now has teeth. Oversight. Veto power. Descendant representation will be written into the charter.

I say yes, and I say why. "Because sunlight is maintenance," I tell them. "And I'm very good at keeping the lights on."

When the call ends, Eric laughs softly. "You realize you just agreed to more work."

"I know."

"Still worth it?"

I look across the road. No fence. No tape. Just land that has learned it won't be left alone again.

"Yes," I say. "Because they can't put this back."

Night settles without pressure. The cicadas sing uninterrupted.

Somewhere, a child reads a name they heard for the first time and decides to ask where it came from.

Silence doesn't answer.

We do.

Chapter Thirty-Nine

What Remains After Witness

The hearing fills the civic center past capacity.

Not with protestors. With families. Strollers line the walls. Folding chairs scrape closer together. Elders sit where they can see and be seen. Descendants wear names on paper pinned to shirts or written on hands, small enough to be intimate, large enough to be legible.

This is what changes the room before a word is spoken.

Eric sits beside me at the long table, a stack of folders neatly aligned, his calm a steady counterweight to the restless energy rolling through the crowd. The county seal hangs behind us, neutral and inadequate.

When the chair gavels the meeting to order, the sound doesn't quiet the room so much as focus it.

"We're here to consider permanent protections for the Angola site," she begins, practiced and careful. "And to hear testimony." The phrase *hear testimony* lands differently now. It doesn't mean performance. It means record.

The first speaker is a hydrologist. She explains springs and flow, and the irreversible harm rushed testing can do. Charts appear. Numbers matter, even here.

Then an archaeologist. Then, a county worker names the shortcuts taken and the protocols skipped.

And then the descendants step forward, one by one. No rush. No theatrics.

A man reads from a letter written by his great-great-grandmother, the paper so fragile he doesn't unfold it fully. A woman speaks about a family rule—*never stop near open water at night*—and how she finally understands why. A teenager reads names from a phone screen, voice shaking only once.

When it's my turn, I don't bring notes.

"We've talked about protection," I say. "And about process. I want to talk about permanence."

The room stills.

"Permanent doesn't mean finished. It means accountable. It means the site isn't managed solely for convenience, quiet, or tourism. It means descendant authority isn't symbolic. It means names stay attached to place."

I let that sit.

"If you fence memory, it breaks. If you share stewardship, it holds."

The chair nods slowly, writing something down.

A motion is introduced. Then another. Language is amended in real time. Descendant veto authority passes by a narrow margin.

An oversight board is formalized. Archaeology is approved with conditions—*non-invasive first, descendant-led consultation mandatory.*

Process does what process can do when it's watched.

Afterward, outside in the late light, people linger again—not because they're afraid to leave, but because they don't want to rush what they just built.

Eric exhales. "They listened."

"They heard," I correct. "Listening comes later."

We walk to the springs before dusk. No stage. No microphones. Just water and people who know why they're there. Someone starts reading names again, quietly this time, like a benediction rather than a demand.

Josiah doesn't come. Not because he's gone. Because he doesn't need to.

The air is light enough to stand on its own.

As the sun drops, I understand something I hadn't before: resolution isn't silence returning. It's noise changing shape. From resistance to care. From warning to work.

At home, I pin a new syllabus to the corkboard. The title reads: "Florida: Land, Water, Memory." Beneath it, a unit header: **1821 — Angola and the Saltwater Railroad**.

Eric watches from the doorway. "You okay?"

"Yes," I say. "Tired. But the good kind."

He smiles. "The kind that lasts."

Across the road, the springs carry evening south, steady and unafraid, no fence to argue with, no shadow pressing in.

Just land that has learned what happens when witnesses stay.

And a story that will not be put back—because too many people know where to stand now, and how to say the names without asking permission.

Chapter Forty

What Grows After the Ground Holds

The consequences arrive quietly.

That's how I know they're real.

Not the theatrical backlash we braced for. Not the sudden reversal that would have made for more straightforward storytelling. Instead, emails that don't get answered anymore. Invitations that stop coming. A few doors that close without explanation.

I noticed it first at a conference in Orlando.

A panel on regional history. My name is still on the program, but my seat has moved from the center to the edge. A moderator who thanks me for my *passion* and then redirects every difficult question toward safer ground.

Afterward, a colleague pulls me aside. "You made some people uncomfortable."

"I hope so," I say. "That's how learning starts."

She smiles, but it's careful. "Just—protect yourself."

Protection now looks like limits.

I say no more often. I choose where I speak. I insist on written agreements, descendant voices, and clarity before collaboration. It costs me some opportunities.

It gives me others.

The park changes shape slowly.

A boardwalk is rerouted to avoid fragile ground. Interpretive signs are rewritten—not smoothed, not softened. Names included. Language direct. A descendant advisory council meets monthly beneath a pavilion that finally feels like it belongs to the land instead of hovering above it.

The springs don't become a shrine. They become a place.

Children wade at the edges. Elders sit in the shade and tell stories that don't lower their voices anymore. A guide reads a name aloud during a tour and doesn't rush past it.

That matters.

At school, the work deepens.

Students interview grandparents. They bring in family trees that suddenly branch south instead of north. One boy turns in a project mapping escape routes not as lines of flight, but as acts of engineering and courage. This matters.

"This was resistance," he writes. "Not running."

I write *yes* in the margin, hard enough to dent the page.

Eric changes, too.

The compliance files finally close—no fanfare, no apology. He keeps the folder anyway, tucked into a drawer he doesn't open often.

"Proof," he says. "That systems remember what you make them carry."

We walk more now. Not always to the springs. Sometimes, just around the block, the ordinary rhythm of days settling back in. We talk about the future without flinching.

"Do you ever wish we'd stopped earlier?" he asks one night.

I think of the fence. The names. The way the land breathed when it was finally allowed to speak.

"No," I say. "But I'm glad we didn't do it alone."

Healing doesn't arrive like forgiveness.

It arrives like work that no longer feels impossible.

Like grief that can be spoken about without breaking something, like memory that no longer demands urgency, only care.

One evening, as the light fades, I walk to the springs by myself. I don't call for Josiah. I don't need to.

But I feel him anyway—not as presence, not as weight. As permission. As the ground that knows it's being tended now.

"Thank you," I say—not to him alone, but to the work, to the people, to the stubborn refusal to let silence win.

The water moves south, carrying reflection and moonlight and the faint echo of names that no longer have to fight to be heard.

This is the future.

Not clean. Not finished.

But held.

And that, I've learned, is enough.

Chapter Forty-One
What Endures

The last marker goes in without ceremony. No crowd. No speeches. Just a small crew, a descendant representative, and a worker who waits until the ground settles before stepping back. The metal catches the late light and holds it, steady and unafraid.

ANGOLA

A maroon settlement.

A place of refuge, resistance, and departure.

Destroyed in 1821. Remembered still.

I stand at the edge of the path with Eric, our shoulders touching, the quiet between us comfortable now. The cicadas begin their evening song right on time. No pause. No warning.

"That's it?" he asks softly.

"That's enough," I answer.

We walk to the springs one last time before dusk claims the day. The water moves the way it always has—patient, southbound, carrying more than it shows. Children skim stones. An elder traces a name with a finger on a smooth rock and leaves it there without explanation.

Memory has learned how to live alongside life.

At school, the year closes with questions instead of summaries. Students don't ask what to memorize; they ask what to listen for. They argue—respectfully, fiercely—about sources and power and whose voice gets to anchor the page.

That's how I know the work took root.

The calls still come. Some are careful. Some are sincere. Some want to package what happened into something tidy and exportable.

I say yes when it feels right. I say no when it doesn't.

Silence hasn't vanished. It never does. It lingers in budgets and delays, in the temptation to soften edges for comfort. But it no longer owns the center of the story.

It has to circle now.

Eric and I sit on the porch as night settles, the road quiet, the park breathing evenly across from us.

"Do you miss him?" he asks.

I consider the question—not with grief, not with longing. With gratitude. "I carry him," I say. "That's different."

Somewhere between the trees and the water, I feel it—not a presence stepping forward, not a voice asking to be heard. Just a steadiness. A sense of rightness that doesn't need explanation. Josiah doesn't need to stand watch anymore. Neither do I.

The Saltwater Railroad isn't a legend now. It's a lesson—about movement, about survival, about what people build when they refuse to be contained by the page.

The future doesn't arrive cleanly. It arrives like this—imperfect, shared, held by many hands instead of one.

Across the springs, moonlight slides south, uninterrupted.

I say the names once more—not aloud, not for anyone else. To know they're there. And then I let the night do what it's always done best—carry the truth forward.

Acknowlegments

With grateful thanks to the following article by Adam Wasserman and to Peter Spalding for his understanding of late suppers and his careful editing.

Thank you to Jeanelle Havlin for her help in formatting. I can never get it right.

To all my fellow authors and friends for their support and encouragement. It means the world to me.

late April 1821: U.S. Attack on Maroon Community at Angola

By Adam Wasserman

Most Black Seminole historians have accounted for the "Negro Fort" and the towns on the Suwannee River in the second decade of the nineteenth century. Still, until recently, an equally substantial settlement that formed in southwest Florida had gone all but ignored. Some of the first Africans arrived in the region as early as the 1770s and 1780s, amidst the War of Independence. In the first two decades of the nineteenth century, each act of American aggression brought new and larger waves of Black and Seminole refugees. The first wave occurred amidst the Patriot invasion of Bowlegs' and Payne's towns in the Seminole capital of Alachua. In January 1813, shortly before the Patriots made the final assault on Alachua, Creek Agent Benjamin Hawkins reported that the Seminoles and Blacks were already retreating to southwest Florida in advance:

I received the following information from an Indian of note. Paine is dead of his wounds . . . the warring Indians have quit this settlement, and gone down to Tellaugue Chapcopopeau, a creek which enters the ocean south of Moscheto river, at a place called the Fishery. Such of their stock as they could command have been driven in that direction, and the negroes were going the same way. The lands beyond the creek towards Florida point were, for a considerable distance, open savannas with ponds; and, still beyond the land, stony to the point.[1]

Hawkins later reported: "The negroes now separated and at a distance from the Indians on the Hammocks or the Hammock not far from Tampa Bay," after they fled the Patriot invasion. More specifically, Hawkins was referring to the Peace River, which flows into Charlotte Harbor near present-day Punta Gorda. "Tellaugue Chapcopopeu" was the Creek town of Talakchopco, located on the main crossing point of the Peace River, present-day Fort Meade in Polk County. The "Fishery" Hawkins mentioned was Charlotte Harbor, where one of the six Cuban *ranchos* on the southwest coast was established. Two hundred men operated these sites during the fishing season from November to April — a multiethnic conglomeration of Spanish, Seminoles, Creeks, and Black Seminoles. For years, many natives from all across the Southeast would travel down to southwest Florida during the winter to these plentiful hunting grounds and exchange deerskins and other crafted items for trade goods with the ranchos. The Seminoles were part of this movement and profited by servicing parties passing into and out of the hunting grounds at Talakchopco. It was likely that their Black maroon allies were familiar with the location as well. After the destruction of their towns in Alachua, Talakchopco served as a primary area of refuge and relief for the destitute Seminoles and Red Sticks. At the same time, their Black allies established themselves in a separate location to the north.[2]

The second wave came with the attack on Prospect Bluff. In 1815, after Nichols left the "Negro Fort," some of the Blacks no longer felt secure in the absence of the British military. Woodbine left the "Negro Fort" with about eighty Blacks who relocated to the region for safety. John Forbes &

Company complain of their runaway slaves having left the area to both Tampa Bay and the Suwannee River after the fort's destruction. John Forbes went down to Tampa Bay to look for these fugitives and found that they were settled around Charlotte Harbor. This community was referred to as "Angola" by Cuban fishermen and became the last remaining stronghold for the Black maroons in Florida after Jackson's invasion. Its precise location was near the Oyster River (present-day Manatee River), a tributary of Sarasota Bay, in Sarasota. In 1821, a South Florida expedition mapped out the region. The map chart was entitled: "A draft of Sarrazota, or Runaway Negro Plantations."[3]

The third refugee wave came with Jackson's assault on Miccosukee and the Suwannee. With Jackson's destruction of Black and native power in northern Florida, various Black, Seminole, Red Stick, and Spanish settlements were established on the southwest Florida coast, stretching from Tampa Bay down to the Peace River. Red Stick leader Peter McQueen and his followers found refuge at Talakchopco. His ally, Chief Opponey, established himself to the north at Lake Hancock, where the

Peace River originates, and his Black followers to the southeast at the town of Minatti. Following Jackson's assault on Suwannee, an 1819 report observed that "the negroes of Sahwanne fled with the Indians of Bowleg's Town toward Chuckachatte" north of Tampa Bay.[4] Captain James Gadsden, aide to Jackson in his Florida campaign, reported back to Jackson about the importance of establishing Tampa Bay as a maritime depot:

It is the last rallying spot of the disaffected negroes and Indians and the only favorable point from whence a communication can be had with Spanish and European emissaries. Nichols, it is reported, has an establishment in that neighborhood, and the negroes and Indians driven from Miccosukee and Suwaney towns have directed their march to that quarter.[5]

At its height, Angola's population grew to become one of the largest maroon towns in the history of Florida. The accounts of the Creek raid on Angola, which recorded the combined number of refugees with enslaved captives, suggest that its population numbered at least around nine hundred at the time of its destruction. Angola was desirable for more than its distance. The Manatee River was an ideal site for trade with Havana and Bahamian merchants. Its proximity to the Spanish *ranchos* ensured that the Blacks would have access to foreign markets for their agricultural goods, fish, and timber, which, in turn, provided Blacks and Seminoles with arms and powder. Besides the fishing ranchos at Tampa Bay and Charlotte Harbor, Cuban fishermen had also established a rancho on the Oyster River in 1812. According to one report of Tampa Bay: "This is an extensive bay, and capable of admitting ships of any size, contiguous to which are the finest lands in East Florida, which Woodbine pretends belong to him by virtue of a grant from the Indians."[6]

Angola's location also made communication and diplomacy with the Spanish and British empires easier. In 1817, there were intelligence reports that Woodbine was amassing a large regiment of Seminole and Black allies in Tampa Bay for the purpose of invading and seizing St. Augustine. This was reportedly intended to prevent the United States from acquiring the territory, rather than out of direct animosity toward Spanish rule. The rumors never materialized. Arbuthnot and Ambrister, the two British officials executed under Jackson's orders, had supported the Blacks at Angola with weapons and trade under Woodbine's orders. Robert Ambrister was commissioned to ensure that the Blacks that Woodbine left at Angola were secure. A witness at his trial reported: "I frequently heard him say he came to attend to Mr. Woodbine's business at the bay of Tamper." The same with Arbuthnot: "The prisoner was sent by Woodbine to Tampa, to see about those negroes he had left there." In 1837, John Lee Williams made observations of ruins left behind from the Angola community as he explored the Oyster River: "The point between these two rivers is called Negro Point. The famous Arbuthnot and Ambrister had at one time a plantation here cultivated by two hundred negroes. The ruins of their cabins and domestic utensils are still seen on the old fields."[7]

Jackson set his sights on the Red Stick and Black refugees almost immediately. In August, several months after his 1818 invasion, Jackson ordered General Gaines to "proceed to, take, and garrison,

Fort St. Augustine with American troops, and hold the garrison prisoners until you hear from the President of the United States." He also ordered Gaines to destroy a settlement of Red Stick followers of Peter McQueen that had returned to the Suwannee River: "I trust before this reaches you, you will destroy the settlement collected at Suwany; this can easily be done by a coup de main, provided secrecy of your movements be observed, and great expedition of march used." Fearing a potential war with Spain over Jackson's aggression, Secretary of War John C. Calhoun countermanded his orders in regards to seizing St. Augustine. He wrote to Gaines: "orders in relation to St. Augustine were given . . . You will accordingly not carry that part of Jackson's order into execution." Yet Calhoun did not repudiate Jackson's command to strike the Red Stick settlement assembled on the Suwannee River. Jackson's determination to obliterate remaining pockets of Black and native resistance in Florida, as well as Calhoun's willingness to look the other way out of sympathy with his objectives, would lead to devastating consequences.[8]

To be sure, the Monroe Administration held many of the same objectives as Jackson: U.S. expansion into Florida and Manifest Destiny, dispossessing the Florida natives and enslaving the Blacks among them, and expanding slavery into Florida. However, they approached matters more cautiously than Jackson. In turn, Jackson, whose temper flared over the "inaction" of the government, made clear his opposition to the "timid, temporizing course of policy" of the Monroe Administration. While sharing Jackson's objectives, the more sophisticated elites of the ruling class understood that diplomacy and patience were often more effective than results-driven aggression. But the political discourse on Manifest Destiny, Indian Removal, and slavery expansion remained within tight perimeters, which entailed merely debating the most effective methods on how to achieve these mutually desirable ends. Many also feared that Jackson was becoming too powerful. Addressing Jackson's fury at being restricted from taking over Florida, Calhoun's reply reflected both of these concerns:

I concur in the view which you have taken . . . and such, I believe, is the opinion of every member of the administration . . . it appears to me that a certain degree of caution ought, at this time, to mark our policy. A war with Spain... such a war would not continue long without involving other parties . . . if it can be prudently and honorably avoided for the present, it ought to be. We want time to grow, to perfect our fortifications, to enlarge our navy, to replenish our depots, and to pay our debts. I speak to you frankly, knowing your zeal for our country, whose glory yours is now identified. No one who has examined my political discourse will, I am sure, think that timid councils influence these opinions.[9]

In the meantime, pro-white Creeks were making plans to enslave the Blacks among the Florida natives when the time was right. On October 2, 1818, Creek Indian Agent David B. Mitchell, the former Governor of Georgia, met with several Creek chiefs, including Coweta chief William McIntosh, at his home in Midgeville, Georgia. After discussing plans for the relocation of the Florida natives into the Creek Nation, Mitchell later summarized a part of the meeting: "In the event of their removal [from Florida] I have it in contemplation to Send McIntosh with a Party of warriors to capture and bring away all the Negroes . . . but, if he goes he will expect it to be in the Service of the U States."[10]

As if anticipating a last stand, Blacks at Angola began accumulating weapons from their Spanish and British allies. Col. Robert Butler reported that the natives and Blacks were fortifying themselves at Tampa Bay. With reports of Spanish provision of armaments for Blacks and natives at Tampa Bay, General Gaines offered to "do what can be done with the limited means under my control, and strike at any force that may present itself." In November, it was reported that the natives had also procured "some provisions and ammunition" from "an English trading vessel" at Tampa Bay. According to the report, the Spanish "furnished hostile Indians, at the bay of Tampa, with ten horseloads of ammunition, recommending to them united and vigorous operations against us."[11]

Jackson remained adamant in his goal to destroy independent Black, Seminole, and Red Stick settlements throughout the peninsula. In a letter to Calhoun in November 1818, only three months after the previous, Jackson proposed establishing a fort and increasing the military force in Tampa with five or six hundred regulars to "ensure permanent tranquility in the south." This detachment was primarily intended to destroy "Woodbine's negro establishment." Afterwards, this regiment would move up and station at Picolata on the St. John's River, proceeding westward to the Suwannee, forcing the submission of all "hostile Indians" along the way, who would then be removed out of Florida and to the Creek Nation. Calhoun failed to authorize the request. Angola had secured itself for the time being.[12]

Aside from procuring arms, the Seminoles and Blacks directly petitioned for British and Spanish support. On September 29, 1819, a body of twenty-eight Seminole delegates led by Miccosukee chief Kinache landed on New Providence Island, Bahamas, to solicit the British for assistance. A close ally to head chief Micanopy, Kinache interpreter, described as an "Indian with mixed blood," may have been the Black Seminole leader

Abraham. Having consistently allied with the British on the Florida frontier, the Seminoles had every reason to believe that they would come to their aid. "They represent themselves as driven from their homes and hunted as wild deer," one correspondent reported, "that there are about 2000 of them, and that their greatest enemies are the Cowetas, a nation like themselves, who, having made terms with the Americans, are set on by them to harass and annihilate their tribe." But fearful of upsetting friendly relations with the U.S. government, the British officials at Nassau declined their request. After being fed and housed for a week, Kinache and his followers were returned to Florida. But evidence of Edward Nicholls' presence at Angola suggests that the British official, despite Nassau's official policy, was committed to the promises he had made to help protect the natives and Blacks back in 1815. A year later, four groups of "South Florida Indians" arrived at Havana, comprised of six chiefs and 120 natives from the "coast of Tampa." Nothing is mentioned about the Spanish agreeing to come to their aid [13]

In February 1819, Spain ceded Florida to the United States in the Adams-Onis Treaty. The pact included a provision that guaranteed protection and rights for the inhabitants of the territory:

The inhabitants of the Territories which His Catholic Majesty cedes to the United States by this Treaty, shall be incorporated in the Union of the United States, as soon as may be consistent with the principles of the Federal Constitution, and admitted to the enjoyment of all privileges, rights, and immunities of the Citizens of the United States [14]

While this provision would temporarily allow the free Blacks of St. Augustine and Pensacola to retain their freedom under the slave regime, little regard was given to the Black maroons and Seminoles. In fact, the five million dollars went mostly to Floridian slaveholders who claimed the loss of slaves into Seminole territory, essentially making the fugitive slaves and Black Seminoles property of the Federal government. This treaty provision had various loopholes. Georgian whites did not consider the Seminoles as independent from the Creek Nation and were thus not the "true inhabitants" of Florida. This official doctrine, to be used or discarded selectively, ignored the fact that the Seminoles had established their independence from the Creeks over 70 years earlier, and that Seminole independence had been a slow process of autonomy on the periphery of the Creek Federation. The policy makers insisted that the Seminoles were outlaws who had "run away" from the Creek Federation. The U.S. government would hold the Creeks accountable for the Seminoles, attempting to enforce dubious reparations through a treaty. Whites could also work their way around the Adams-Onis treaty by claiming that the Black Seminoles were recent runaways rather than residents who had established themselves in Florida for over a century.

In January 1821, the Creeks ceded five million acres of their best land through the Treaty of Indian Springs in exchange for $450,000 in annual payments to the Creek Nation over a period of 14 years. However, the Creeks were forced to pay $250,000 out of their annuity to the state of Georgia as reparations for claims of "lost property" of runaway slaves in Seminole territory. On

December 29, 1820, the Georgia treaty commissioners delivered a "talk" to the Creek chief council regarding fugitive slaves: "As the negroes now remaining among the Seminoles, now belonging to the white people, we consider those people (the Seminoles) a part of the Creek nation; and we look for the chiefs of the Creek nation to cause the people there, as well as the people of the Upper Towns, to do justice." William McIntosh spoke to the Georgia commissioners regarding fugitive slaves: "If the President admits that country [Florida] to belong to the Creek nation, he will take his warriors, go down, and bring all he can get, and deliver them up."[15] The treaty entirely transformed the Coweta Creeks into determined slave-raiders. They legally claimed the Blacks in Seminole territory as their own property and would feature among the primary antagonists towards their freedom from this point forward. Despite receiving compensation for their fugitives, Floridian and Georgian slaveholders would continue to push claims of ownership of Blacks in Seminole territory as well. Although having already compensated both, the Federal government continued to support their claims by agitating natives to hand over the fugitives and Blacks among them.

When the Adams-Onis treaty took effect on February 1821, President Monroe appointed Andrew Jackson the territory's first governor, an unsettling development for the Red Sticks and Blacks of Angola to put it mildly. On April 2, 1821, Andrew Jackson requested Secretary of State John Quincy Adams for the President's instructions regarding the Red Stick Creek settlements scattered along the peninsula, "and likewise in relation to the negroes who have run away from the States, and inhabit the country, and are protected by the Indians." Adams forwarded the request to the Secretary of War, John C. Calhoun. On May 1, Calhoun declined Jackson's request and ordered him to take no immediate measures.[16]

In typical Jackson form, he took action before receiving an answer. In late April, Chief William McIntosh ordered a war party of Coweta Creeks to go down into Florida to break up the Red Stick Creek settlements and enslave the Blacks at Angola. This raiding party was composed of two hundred Coweta warriors under the command of chiefs William Weatherford and Charles Miller, well-known as close allies of both McIntosh and Jackson. An "eye-witness," more than likely a participant in the raid, described their objectives in the editorial columns of the Charleston *Gazette*:

Towards the end of April last, some men of influence and fortune, residing somewhere in the western country, thought of making a speculation to obtain enslaved people for a trifle. They hired Charles Miller, William Weatherford [and others], and under these chiefs, were engaged about two hundred Cowetas Indians. They were ordered to proceed south along the western coast of East Florida. They take, in the name of the United States, and make prisoners of all the men of colour, including women and children, they would be able to find, and bring them all, well secured, to a certain place, which has been kept a secret.[17]

The Creek raiders wreaked havoc throughout central Florida until they launched a surprise attack on Angola and devastated the settlement. The raiders captured over three hundred Angola inhabitants, plundered their plantations, and set fire to all of their homes. Afterwards, the war party made its way south to Charlotte Harbor and plundered several Spanish ranchos. Most of the three hundred Blacks captured in the raid disappeared as the Creek party returned to Georgia. The "eye-witness" in the Charleston *Gazette* provided a complete account:

They arrived at Sazazota, surprised and captured about 300 of them, plundered their plantations, set on fire all their houses, and then proceeding southerly captured several others; and on the 17th day of June, arrived at the Spanish Ranches, in Pointerrass Key, in Carlos Bay, where not finding as many Negroes as they expected, they plundered the Spanish fishermen of more than 2000 dollars worth of property, besides committing the most significant excess. With their plunder and prisoners, they returned to the place appointed for the deposit of both.[18]

The aftermath of the raid was chaotic for the Black maroons, Seminoles, and Red Stick Creeks in the Florida territory. Settlements were scattered, refugees fled into different areas, and others, having grown tired of the constant terror of U.S. aggression, escaped from the country. About 300 refugees from Angola left in canoes for the Florida Keys and then sailed to the Bahamas aboard British wrecking vessels. The "eye-witness" narrated the aftermath of the assault:

The terror thus spread along the Western Coast of East Florida broke all the establishments of both Blacks and Indians, who fled in great consternation. The Blacks principally, thought they could not save their lives but by abandoning the country; therefore, they, by small parties and in their Indian canoes, doubled Cape Sable and arrived at Key Taviniere, which is the general place of rendezvous for all the English wreckers [those who profited from recovery of shipwreck property], from Nassau, Providence; an agreement was soon entered into between them, and about 250 of these negroes were by the wreckers carried to Nassau and clandestinely landed.[19]

A Florida observer wrote that some of the blacks from the "Negro Fort," along with runaway slaves from Florida and other Southern states,

formed considerable settlements on the waters of Tampa Bay. When the Indians went in pursuit of these negroes, such as escaped, made their way down to Cape Florida and the reef, about which they collected within a year and a half upwards of three hundred; vast numbers of them have been at different times since carried off by the Bahama wreckers to Nassau [20]

After the assault, some Black residents armed themselves and remained isolated in the state's southwest region under the protection of Spanish traders. Some Florida residents petitioned the President to "retain their property" that escaped to an island or cluster of islands off the Florida west coast and were "protected by an armed banditti."[21] In July, a small party of destitute Seminoles made their way to St. Augustine, informing Capt. John R. Bell that "very recently a party of Indians (Cawetus) said to be headed by McIntosh came into their neighborhood and had taken off a considerable number of negroes and some Indians, that the commander of the party had sent them information that in a short time he should return and drive all the Indians off."[22] Bell denied that the party was authorized by Jackson or any higher authorities, but failed to acknowledge that McIntosh was Jackson's proxy who had served under him in his Florida campaign.

A mass exodus of Black people occurred from the Keys to the Bahamas. James Forbes reported that runaway Blacks were amassed at Cape Florida: "At this key, which presents a mass of mangroves, there were lately about sixty Indians, and as many runaway negroes, in search of sustenance, and twenty-seven sail of Bahaman wreckers."[23] Florida officials were not merely satisfied with the Blacks taken during the Coweta raid. In 1823, Governor William Duval wrote to the Secretary of War in apprehension of fugitive Blacks who had escaped from Angola to Andros Island, Bahamas:

I have been informed by Gentlemen upon whom I can rely, that there are about ninety negros, fugitives from this Province and the neighboring States, on St. Andrews Island one of the Bahamas, & about thirty more on the Great Bahamas & the neighboring Islands, those Negros went from Tampa Bay, & Charlotte Harbour, in boats to the Florida Keys from whence they were taken to the Bahamas by the Providence Wreckers. The enslaved people might be obtained, if Com. Porter is ordered to demand them from the authorities on those Islands.[24]

James Forbes also reported to Secretary of State John Quincy Adams that the Seminoles "apprehend some disturbance from the Cowetas. These last are said to have been at Tampa about 200 strong and taken from thence about 120 Negroes after destroying four Spanish settlements there."[25]

But the raid had not solved the problem that the free Black maroons posed in subjugating Florida natives. In July 1821, Jean A. Penieres, Sub-agent for Indian affairs in Florida, gave the first official account of the problem of Black maroon influence over their Seminole "masters":

We must add to this enumeration. . . . fifty or sixty Negroes, or mulattos, who are maroons, or half slaves to the Indians. These Negroes appeared to me far more intelligent than those who are in absolute slavery, and they have a significant influence over the minds of the Indians. It will be challenging to form a prudent determination with respect to the maroon Negroes who live among the Indians on the other side of the little mountains of

Latchiove. Their number is said to be upward of three hundred. They fear again being enslaved under the American government and will omit nothing to increase or keep alive mistrust among the Indians, whom they in fact govern. If it should become necessary to use force with them, it is to be feared that the Indians will take their part. It will, however, be required to remove from Florida this lawless group of freebooters, among whom runaway Negroes will always find refuge. It would perhaps be possible to have them received at St. Domingo, or furnish them the means of withdrawing themselves from the United States [26]

Responding in September, Jackson concurred with Penieres' proposal to remove the Black Seminoles from Florida. He proposed the establishment of a military base at Picolata to prevent fugitive slaves from escaping into Seminole territory:

This must be done, or the frontier will be much weakened by the Indian settlements and be a perpetual harbor for our slaves. These runaway slaves, spoken of by Mr. Penieres, must be removed from the Floridas, or scenes of murder and confusion will exist and lead to unhappy consequences that can't be controlled.[27]

In August, Creek Agent John Crowell wrote in a letter to Secretary of War John C. Calhoun to inform him of the Coweta raid: "Some short time previous to my coming into this agency, the chiefs, had organized a Regt. of Indian Warriors, and sent them into Florida in pursuit of negroes that had escaped from their owners, in the Creek nation as well as such as had run off from their owners in the States; this detachment has recently returned, bringing with them, to this place fifty nine negroes, besides about twenty delivered to their respective owners on their march up."[28] Failing to mention Jackson's involvement in organizing the incursion, or that the Creek leaders of the raid were Jackson's close allies, Calhoun shouldered the blame entirely on the Cowetas. "The expedition to Florida was entirely unknown to this Department," Calhoun furiously responded in September, "I have to express my concern at, and most decided approbation of, the conduct of the chiefs; that they should seize upon the very moment when that country was about to pass from the possession of

Spain to that of the United States, and when everything was in confusion, to use the superior force of the Creek nation over the weakness of the Seminoles, to impose on and plunder them."[29]

Objecting to the violent Creek raid of fugitive slaves in the Seminole territory, Calhoun wrote to Florida Indian Agent John Bell: "The government expects that the Slaves who have run away or been plundered from our Citizens or from Indian tribes within our limits will be given up peaceably by the Seminole Indians when demanded."[30] This alternative policy of agitating the Seminoles to turn over fugitive slaves would become the primary point of contention between natives and whites on the Florida frontier for the following fifteen years.

Crowell also understood that Calhoun was more concerned with retrieving fugitive slaves than with Seminole impoverishment. He replied to Calhoun in January:

Special orders were given to Col. Miller not to interrupt the person or the property of any Indian or white man & he declares that he did not take from the possession of either red or white person a single negro except one from a vessel belonging to the celebrated Nichols, lying at anchor in Tampa Bay. The negroes he took were found and acknowledged by the inhabitants of the country to be runaways.[31]

Crowell then provided a list of 59 slaves that had made it to the United States from the Creek raid, entitled "Description of the Negroes brought into the Creek nation by a detachment of Indian Warriors under the command of Col. Wm. Miller, a half-breed Indian." In turn, Calhoun provided the list to Capt. John R. Bell, in hopes that some Florida slaveholders could retrieve their property: "I furnished you with a list of negroes taken from the Seminole Indians by a party of Creeks; by which it would seem that many of them belong to the Inhabitants of Florida."[32]

Following the Coweta invasion, slaveholders attempted to retrieve their fugitive slaves who were either seized by the Creek warriors or had fled to the Bahamas. The "eye-witness" in the Charleston *Gazette* rhetorically concluded his editorial column on the Coweta Creek invasion:

Now all these Negroes, as well as those captured by the Indians, and those gone to Nassau, are runaway Slaves, from the Planters on St. John's River, in Florida, Georgia, Carolina, and a few from Alabama. Cannot those Planters who have had their Negroes missing recover them by means of these chiefs I have named, and who are so well known by the parts they have been playing for some time past in the late Indian wars, and discover who are those speculative gentlemen who now hold their Negroes, and if they were lawfully their slaves? Could not all those Negroes unlawfully introduced into Nassau also be recovered by an application to the English governor, backed by a formal demand from the Government of the United States? [33]

But when it came to retrieving the refugee Blacks, Governor Duval's hands were tied. Duval could not pursue the Black refugees from Angola unless he received permission from Bahaman authorities, nor could he call out a militia against the Blacks in Florida territory unless he received Presidential authority. He instructed Captain Horatio S. Dexter, as he toured Central Florida in 1823, to capture any runaway slaves he found in the vicinity of Tampa

Bay and employ an "Indian force" if the slaves resisted. Duval reported that a "considerable number of slaves" had established themselves at Pine Island on the mouth of the Charlotte River after fleeing from Tampa. They were "well armed with Spanish Muskets" and "refused to permit any American to visit the Island." Duval estimated that "more than 1,000" runaways continued to reside in the whole territory. The Blacks at Charlotte Harbor maintained their allegiance to the Spanish traders, cutting timber and fishing for the Havana market. In turn, the Spaniards provided them with protection, deploying several small gunboats armed with one to three guns each. But Duval could not comply with the demands of slavers unless he received Presidential authority, to which he planned to commission sixty mounted militiamen under the command of Col. Gad Humphreys to apprehend the Blacks. [34]

In his 1823 tour of Florida, Dexter found "eighty refugee Negroes belonging to Indians & Citizens of this territory who are established on the sea coast near Tampa where the Havana fishing smacks employ them, & pass to Cuba frequently, the crews of these smacks bring goods to trade with the Indians." Even some Seminoles, Horatio Dexter found, were often "prevented by force" from communicating with the maroon settlements scattered along the inner islands of southwest Florida, "as the Negroes were all completely armed with Spanish musquets, Bayonets & Cartouche boxes." Whenever these crews needed cattle, they landed and exchanged powder, lead, molasses, and rum. The marshes between the islands and the mainland were shallow, some natives told Dexter, and the armed vessels frequently landed "packages of goods at different depots on these Islands." These vessels were generally mounted with one, two, or three large guns. After the U.S. acquisition of Florida, these Cuban traders carried on a constant communication with the West Indies, Dexter reported, "& have been the means of carrying off a number of refugee Negroes belonging to the inhabitants of this Territory and the neighboring States."[35]

The Blacks and Seminoles of Middle and Central Florida also felt the effects of the Creek incursion. From the Suwannee River down to Charlotte

Harbor, the Coweta Creek raiders apprehended fugitive slaves. They broke up numerous settlements, dispersing the impoverished Floridian natives and Blacks into even more remote locations. About ten miles from the Withlacoochee River, Horatio Dexter found that the settlement of Chucachate, which had formerly been the seat of the Seminole Nation, had been "broken up by the incursions of the Cowetas, who carried off or dispersed about 60 Negro Slaves and a large stock of cattle & horses." Many Black Angolan refugees fled to the Peace River headwaters. As Dexter traveled farther south toward the Peace River, he came across the remote settlement of Chief Opponey. A Red Stick ally of Peter McQueen, Opponey had a plantation situated at Lake Hancock, north of present-day Barstow, Polk County. To the south lay McQueen's settlement of Talakchopco. His twenty slaves resided on the southeast side of the lake in the town of Minatti (Manatee), which became Angola's successor. After Opponey's death, he had left his estate to his son Pulepucka, whose town of Apilchapcocha contained forty natives and seventy Blacks. Many of these blacks at Minatti were Angolan refugees who sought even more remote refuge. There Dexter met some of the kin of the late chief Payne, who informed him: "their object in settling in this remote situation was to avoid the frequent incursions of the Cowetas, whose depredations upon the Indians of the Province ought to engage the early attention of the Agent, and be made the subject of complaint to the Agent of the Creek Nation."[36]

In 1822, Dr. William H. Simmons travelled to a Black settlement in the Big Swamp, "accompanied by an Indian Negro, as a guide." En route, he witnessed the effects of the Coweta incursion: "the sites of Indian towns, which had been recently broken up, and the crops left standing on the ground." These were "chiefly the settlements of Lower Creeks," which had recently "dispersed themselves, or retired to remote situations." At the Big Swamp settlement, Simmons also found that his Black Seminole hosts had recently fled from their homes in apprehension of the Coweta slave raiders, impoverished and unable to provide him with much hospitality:

These people were in the greatest poverty, and had nothing to offer me; having, not long before, fled from a settlement farther west, and left their crop ungathered, from an apprehension of being seized on by the Cowetas, who had recently carried off a body of Negroes, residing near the Suwanee.[37]

The Coweta invasion, compounded with Jackson's invasion, left the Seminoles and Blacks in absolute destitution. Simmons found that "the seizure under the American authority, of a number of fugitive slaves, who had located themselves on the mouth of the Suwanee," had caused many to abandon their settlements and disperse themselves in the woods, leaving their crops to perish on the ground "which, together with the previous loss of their stocks of cattle during the war, had reduced many of them to a state of absolute famine." Simmons found that the Blacks had grown even more militantly opposed to the United States. As he travelled, with his Black Seminole guide, en route from the Ocklawaha River to the Withlacoochee, he grew notably nervous in the company of several other Blacks who were going the same way: "As many of these Negroes were refugee slaves, and some had been soldiers under Woodbine, and fought against the Americans, I did not feel perfectly safe, while travelling in such company, through swamps and obscure paths, in the Seminole country."[38]

U.S. imperialism in Florida led to the increasing decentralization of Black and native settlements. This would, paradoxically, make U.S. efforts to concentrate them within the reservation even more difficult several years later. Native and Black people who had once flourished on the Alachua savannah for almost a century were broken up by the Patriots' invaders. Native and Black people who had once cultivated the fertile banks of the Apalachicola River were broken up by a U.S. incursion that slaughtered hundreds at the "Negro Fort." Native and Black people who cultivated fields along the Suwannee River were broken up by Andrew Jackson's invasion two years later. Native and Black people who lived off the fertile lands and abundant hunting grounds in southwest Florida were broken up by a pro-white Coweta Creek incursion dispatched by Jackson. In four separate incursions over the span of a decade, the U.S. made it clear that its Florida policy was to subjugate its free Black residents to make it safe for slavery to flourish in the territory. Florida was no longer the safeguard of freedom it once was. Following closely behind the Angolan refugees, Simmons found that many Black maroons and free Blacks in St. Augustine were now fleeing out of Florida to Havana:

The indulgent treatment of their slaves, by which the Spaniards are so honourably distinguished: and the ample and humane code of laws which they have enacted, and also enforce, for the protection of the blacks, both bond and free, occasioned many of the enslaved Indians, who were apprehensive of falling into the power of the Americans, and also most of the free people of colour who resided in St. Augustine, to transport themselves to Havana, as soon as they heard of the approach of the American authorities.[39]

This post is a revised excerpt from A People's History of Florida 1513-1876: How Africans,

Seminoles, Women, and Lower Class Whites Shaped the Sunshine State *by Adam Wasserman.*

Footnotes

1. ASPIA, I, 838
2. Louis F. Hayes, *Letters of Benjamin Hawkins, 1797-1815* (Atlanta: Georgia Department of Archives and History, 1939), 198-200; Canter Brown, Jr., *Florida's Peace River Frontier* (Orlando, FL: University of Central Florida Press, 1991), 7-9; Canter Brown, Jr., "Tales of Angola: Free Blacks, Red Stick Creeks, and International Intrigue in Spanish Southwest Florida, 1812-1821," in *Go Sound the Trumpet! Selections of Florida's African American History*, David H. Jackson, Jr., and Canter Brown, Jr., eds. (University of Tampa Press, 2005), 7-8; E.A. Hammond, "The Spanish Fisheries of Charlotte Harbor," *Florida Historical Quarterly* 51 (April 1973), 355-80; James W. Covington, "Trade Relations Between Southwestern Florida and Cuba, 1600-1840," *Florida Historical Quarterly* 38 (Oct. 1959), 115-129.
3. William S. Coker and Thomas D. Watson, *Indian Traders of the Southeastern Spanish Borderlands: Panton, Leslie & Company and John Forbes & Company, 1783-1847* (Pensacola: University of West Florida Press, 1986), 301-302, 309, 320; For a complete illustration of the Angola community see, Canter Brown, Jr., "Sarrazota, or runaway Negro plantations": Tampa Bay's First Black

Community," *Tampa Bay History* 12 (Fall-Winter): 5-19; For examples of references to Sarasota as Angola by Cuban settlers and fishermen see, Walter P. Fuller, "Who was the Frenchman of Frenchman's Creek?" *Tequesta* 29 (1969), 47-48.

4. Young, "A Topographical Memoir," 97.

5. "The Defenses of the Floridas, Report of Capt. James Gadsden," 49.

6. ASPFA, 4, 603; Brown, *Peace River Frontier*, 8.

7. ASPFA, 4, 603, 604; ASPMA, 1, 731; Williams, *Territory of Florida*, 299-300.

8. ASPMA, 1, 744-745.

9. Ibid.

10. James F. Doster, *Creek Indians: The Creek Indians and their Florida Lands, 1740-1823*, 2 vols (New York: Garland, 1974), 231.

11. Clarence Carter, ed., *Territorial Papers of the United States: Territory of Florida*, vols. XXII-XXVI (Washington, DC: 1956-1962), Vol. XXII, 167; ASPMA, 1, 752-753.

12. ASPMA, 1, 752-753.

13. *Niles' Weekly Register*, XVII, 243; Rosalyn Howard, "The "Wild Indians of Andros Island: Black Seminole Legacy in the Bahamas," *Journal of Black Studies* 37 (Nov., 2006), 280; William C. Sturtevant, "Chakaika and the "Spanish Indians": Documentary Sources Compared with Seminole Tradition," *Tequesta* 13 (1953), 38-39.

14. ASPFA, 4, 620.

15. ASPIA, 2, 252-253.

16. ASPFA, 4, 755; Carter, *Territorial Papers*, XXII, 57, 40.

17. "Advice to Southern Planters" in Charleston *Gazette*, c. November 1821, reprinted in Philadelphia *National Gazette and Literary Register*, December 3, 1821, cited in Brown, "Sarrazota, or Runaway Negro Plantations," 13.

18. Ibid.

19. Ibid.

20. Vignoles, Charles B. *Observations upon the Floridas*. New York: E. Bliss & E. White, 1823: 135-136.

21. Carter, *Territorial Papers*, XXII, 763.

22. Ibid. 126

23. Forbes, *Sketches, Historical and Topographical, of the Floridas*, 105.

24. Carter, *Territorial Papers*, XXII, 745.

25. Ibid. 119.

26. ASPIA, 2, 411-412.

27. Ibid. 414.

28. John Crowell to John C. Calhoun, August 20, 1821, in T. J. Peddy, *Creek Letters 1820-1824* (typescript in Georgia Department of Archives and History, Atlanta), 21.8.20.C.C.

29. J.C. Calhoun to John Crowell, September 29, 1821, *Creek Letters 1820-1824*, 21.9.29.C.C.

30. Carter, *Territorial Papers*, XXII, 219.

31. John Crowell to J.C. Calhoun, January 22, 1822, *Creek Letters 1820-1824*, 22.1.22.C.C.

32. Carter, *Territorial Papers*, XXII, 221.

33. Cited in Brown, "Sarrazota, or Runaway Negro
    Plantations," 13.

34. Carter, *Territorial Papers*, XXII, 681, 744.

35. Boyd, Mark F. "Horatio Dexter and Events Leading to
    the Treaty of Moultrie Creek with the Seminole
    Indians." *Florida Anthropologist* 11 (September 1958):
    81, 87, 92-93.

36. Ibid. 89, 82, 92-93; Brown, "Tales of Angola," 12.

37. Simmons, *Notice of East Florida*, 41-42.

38. Ibid. 84, 44.

39. Ibid. 42.

About the Author

Brenda Spalding is a talented writer who has received several awards. Her expertise in publishing and marketing makes her a regular guest speaker at writers' conferences, book clubs, and writers' groups.

The author is a past president of the National League of American Pen Women- Sarasota Branch, a member of the Sarasota Fiction Writers, Florida Authors and Publishers Association, and the Florida Writers Association, and on the board of directors for the Florida Writers Foundation. She is an adviser to the not-for-profit ICreate LLC in Sarasota.

www.brendaspaldingauthor.com
spaldingauthor@gmail.com

www.ingramcontent.com/pod-product-compliance
Lightning Source LLC
Chambersburg PA
CBHW061100100726
47911CB00012B/326